THE TOWERING NOVEL OF WONDROUS EXCITEMENT

—NOW A MAJOR MOVIE FROM WALT DISNEY STUDIOS!

ISLAND AT THE TOP
OF THE WORLD

IAN CAMERON

Formerly titled
THE LOST ONES

AVON
PUBLISHERS OF BARD, CAMELOT, DISCUS, EQUINOX AND FLARE BOOKS

AVON BOOKS
A division of
The Hearst Corporation
959 Eighth Avenue
New York, New York 10019

ISBN: 0-380-00151-9

First Avon Printing, January, 1970.
Fourth Printing.

AVON TRADEMARK REG. U.S. PAT. OFF. AND
FOREIGN COUNTRIES, REGISTERED TRADEMARK—
MARCA REGISTRADA, HECHO EN CHICAGO, U.S.A.

Printed in the U.S.A.

ISLAND AT THE TOP
OF THE WORLD

Contents

	Introduction	ix
1	"Missing, Believed Killed"	13
2	The Graveyard of the Whales	20
3	An Expedition Is Formed	32
4	Flight North	38
5	Into the Unknown	45
6	"We're Being Watched!"	54
7	A Whisper of Aspen Leaves	70
8	"Where the Caribou Can Lead, We Can Follow"	82
9	The Girl with the "Bewitchen Sent of FlowerS"	99
10	Escape	111
11	The Last of the Vikings	126
12	In Such Stillness the World Was Born	132
13	The Mouth of Hell	138
14	"My Son, My Son"	149
15	The Guardians	159
16	No Way Out	167
17	"Greater Love Hath No Man than This . . ."	178
18	The Reward	188

Introduction

NOBODY, I am told, reads an Introduction nowadays, and when I said I was going to write one, the various friends who are "helping" me over my story all threw up their hands in horror; it just wasn't done, they said. However, I feel that some sort of explanation is called for about both the contents and style of *The Lost Ones*, and an Introduction strikes me as being the right and proper place in which to make it.

As regards the contents, it was never my intention to write a full account of everything we did and saw during our nine months in the Arctic. We met with so many strange adventures, that several things on which I should have liked to dwell at length are hardly mentioned. I should have liked, for example, to say much more about the fair-haired Eskimoes of the Parry Islands, and of the scientific evidence which, according to the experts, proves beyond doubt that they are descended from the Viking colonists of Greenland. I should have liked to digress a little on the subject of the curious habits of the Sperm whale —animals which are surely the most amazing of all created creatures having, to mention only one of their peculiarities, lop-sided heads (a third the length of their bodies) which contain a vast hydrostatic buoyancy chamber used to control their breathing during deep-water dives. Several pages, too, might have been given to a consideration of Arctic *flora*; indeed, I doubt if Professor Somerville will ever forgive me for failing to mention the many rare and beautiful flowers which we came across during our travels. But the truth of the matter is this. It seemed to me that the best thing would be to relate our adventures in a plain straightforward manner, leaving all technical and scientific details to be explained later.

As to the style of the story, I can only apologize for it. I have spent nearly all my fifty-two years in the Arctic, trapping, gold-prospecting, hunting and whaling; so it is not to be wondered at if I turn out to be handier with a rifle than a pen. However, I am encouraged by an old whalers' saying, "A good harpoon needs no honing"; perhaps on the same principle, a true story, if it is strange and exciting enough (and ours is certainly that), needs no embellishments. At any rate, in this hope I will get under way.

KEITH ROGERS

Pangnirtung, Baffin Island
Spring 1960

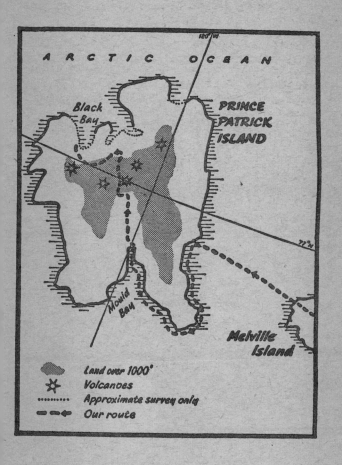

A R C T I C   O C E A N

180° W

Black
Bay

PRINCE
PATRICK
ISLAND

Mould
Bay

77° N

Melville
Island

Land over 1000'

Volcanoes

Approximate survey only

Our route

1

"Missing, Believed Killed"

I FIRST met the captain and his friend Professor Somerville aboard the S.S. *Dunvegan*, an ancient cargo-cum-passenger liner running between Quebec and Baffin Island. It came about like this.

I had just spent a most frustrating spring hunting walrus along the shore of the Hudson Bay. Everything went wrong that trip; the mosquitoes were thick as a plague of locusts, the walrus were late in reaching their breeding grounds, and to cap it all the launch I had hired foundered off Richmond Gulf and I lost the best part of all my ivory. Feeling that this was the last straw, I decided to cut my losses, trek across to the Labrador coast, and pick up the *Dunvegan* as she headed north on her annual run to the whaling station at Pangnirtung—once there, there'd be plenty of jobs I could take my pick of.

Well, to cut a long story short, the *Dunvegan* and I fetched up at Hamilton Inlet on the same day, and I duly boarded her and settled down to enjoy a ten-days' voyage up one of the most beautiful coasts in the world—beautiful, that is, when viewed from the deck of a steamer; when trekking up it by sledge I can think of other adjectives to describe it!

Most of the *Dunvegan*'s passengers I found I could

place at a glance. There was the usual crowd of whalers bound for the refinery at Pangnirtung; a handful of traders working for the Company (the Hudson's Bay Company, that is); a couple of Grenfell Mission doctors likely to do a great deal of good wherever they went; and a party of uranium survey experts likely, I suspect, to do nothing of the sort. But two of the passengers baffled me; I couldn't place them at all. By referring to the passenger list I discovered their names, Captain Anthony McIver, R.N., and Professor James D. Somerville; also the fact that they were booked right through to Pangnirtung. But of the business that was taking them far into the Arctic I could obtain no clue.

The captain, whom I picked out by his naval duffel-coat, was a tall, good-looking man, a shade the wrong side of forty. He had dark hair, sharply defined features, and grey deep-set eyes. He also had a disconcerting habit of staring very straight at whomever he was talking to; a habit which reminded me of somebody else, though at the time I could not think who.

The professor seemed to be a few years younger than his companion. He was a small, precisely spoken man, very compact in his appearance, and very methodical in everything he did. He appeared to have a great liking for snuff; for even on the windblown deck of the *Dunvegan* I noticed him taking frequent pinches. (I was to discover later that he was not in fact particularly fond of snuff, but took it as a cure for chronic asthma. But this is anticipating.)

We stood out of Hamilton Inlet late in the afternoon, and ran almost at once into a most unpleasant cross-swell. Being flat-bottomed and sailing light, the *Dunvegan* was soon rolling her guts out, and after a couple of hours even the hardened whalers retired *en bloc* to their cabins. For dinner the saloon was practically deserted; but among the few who did put in an appearance were Captain McIver and Professor Somerville, and I found that the three of us had been seated together at the captain's table. This pleased me; for it gave me the chance to make their acquaintance.

During the meal the professor and I soon fell to talking about the Arctic; he asking a great number of questions and I answering as well as I could. He was, I soon discov-

14

ered, an authority on Arctic *flora*, and for some time our conversation centered round the flowers of the tundra, beautiful as butterflies and, alas, almost as short-lived. Then we started talking of whales.

"Ah, sir!" exclaimed the *Dunvegan*'s captain, "you're on a good tack now. Gunner Rogers knows more about whales than any man in the Arctic."

Captain McIver all this while had been listening quietly; but now he leaned forward, staring at me in his peculiar, and, as I have said, strangely reminiscent manner.

"Excuse me, sir," he said, leaning across the table, "but is your name Keith Rogers?"

I said that it was.

The captain made no further comment; but I noticed that he and the professor exchanged glances.

I had intended, as soon as dinner was over, to return to my cabin; but while the coffee was being cleared away Captain McIver suggested that the three of us adjourn to the far end of the lounge—which was almost deserted—for a glass of whisky. The professor and I agreed, and soon we were comfortably settled into the *Dunvegan*'s securely bolted chairs.

"Mr. Rogers," the captain said, when the steward had brought our drinks, "I believe that about a year ago you were somewhere to the west of Lancaster Sound aboard the whaling ship *Northern Harvester?*"

"I was," I replied, surprised that my movements should have been of such apparent interest.

"You were Fangst Leader, I understand?" put in the professor.

"That's right," I said. "I had the job of directing the movements of the whaling fleet."

The captain now leaned forward, watching me with great intentness.

"And do you," he asked, "remember a young man aboard the *Harvester* named Donald Ross?"

I put my whisky back on the table.

"Yes," I said. "I remember Donald Ross."

Again the captain and professor exchanged glances.

"Mr. Rogers," the former said, "we should be very grateful if you would give us a few details about Donald Ross's disappearance."

"I'm sorry," I said, "but I can't."

15

The captain's eyes narrowed as if in pain. He spoke very earnestly.

"I assure you, Mr. Rogers," he said, "I don't ask out of idle curiosity. I have a special reason for wanting to know. A very special reason."

Now I didn't like the turn the conversation had taken. Young Ross's disappearance was a sore point with the whaling company—apart from anything else their helicopter hadn't been insured against theft—and I saw no reason to discuss the affair with strangers.

"Donald Ross," I said slowly, "died in rather mysterious circumstances nearly a year ago. I think the ashes are too cold to be raked over any more."

Again the captain's eyes narrowed in pain.

"Donald Ross," he said, "was my son."

I cursed myself for my lack of perception. Their physique was quite different; their features were no more than vaguely similar; but how could I have failed to associate their common trait; their habit of staring so disconcertingly straight at whoever they were talking to?

"I'm sorry," I said.

It sounded very trite and very inadequate, but the captain seemed to sense that I meant it. He leaned forward.

"Mr. Rogers"—he spoke with quiet determination—"I have come to Canada to find what happened to my son. I know it won't be easy. I know I shall meet with difficulty, non-cooperation and every sort of obstruction. But I want to know the truth. You, sir," and here he fixed me with his disconcerting stare, "were one of the people I hoped would help me."

I pulled out my pipe. It took me several minutes to pack the bowl—a job over which I never like to hurry—and it took me several minutes more to get the pipe drawing sweetly. But even then I hadn't made up my mind.

"I think the best thing," I said at last, "would be if you told me what you already know about your son's disappearance. Afterwards, I'll fill in as many gaps as I can."

I was looking at the captain as I spoke; but at that moment the *Dunvegan* gave a heavier than usual roll, and in the looking-glass at the opposite end of the lounge I saw the reflection of the professor. He was nodding his head in agreement: nodding away like a string-jerked marionette. The captain also reacted favourably.

16

"Mr. Rogers," he said, "you're the first man who hasn't shut up like a clam at the mention of my boy's death. I'm more grateful than I can say." He pulled a sheaf of papers out of his wallet. "Last October," he went on, "I received this telegram." He passed one of the papers across the table.

2.9.58 I read, *ROSS, Dragonfly-Cottage, Bridport, Dorset, U.K. Very much regret your son Donald Ross is missing believed killed. Letter follows immediately. Kinross and Jameson.*

"To say that I was broken-hearted," the captain went on, "would be no exaggeration. My wife died in the war. Donald was our only son; and" —he said it with a moving simplicity—"we loved each other deeply. Very deeply. At first I couldn't believe he was dead. Missing believed killed, you know. gives one a cruel sort of hope. I waited for the whaling company's letter, which, I imagined, would give me details of what had happened. But when the letter came it was a bitter disappointment. It simply told me that my son was dead; that his body hadn't been recovered, and that his personal effects would be sent on to me in due course.

"Now I wanted to know what had happened. Missing believed killed is a turn of phrase that's got to be accepted in war. But in peacetime relatives have a right to be told the facts. Or so it seemed to me. So I wrote to the whaling company asking for details. Their reply was another disappointment: they were sorry but no details were available. Soon after this I called at their head office in Leadenhall Street; and it was here that a vague impression I'd had for some time was confirmed. There was something mysterious about Donald's death: something the whaling company wanted to hide.

"Well, to cut a long story short, they eventually told me my son had been lost in a storm. But"—and here I noticed the captain was watching me closely—"by this time I'd become suspicious. I'd made private inquiries using my first names only: Anthony McIver; and I'd found out that for several days before and after Donald's death the sky had been clear, and the sea had been calm as a millpond. There had been no storm. So I went on making inquiries, and what it all boiled down to was this. Out of all the people I wrote to and talked to, not one could tell me how my son had died. Not one could even tell me, with any certainty, that he had died at all. As far as I could make out he had simply disappeared.

"And so," the captain ended, "I resigned my commission and came out to Canada. And I shall not leave Canada," he added, "until I know what happened to my son."

I had been listening to Captain McIver—or rather to Captain McIver Ross as I now knew him to be—with the greatest attention. His story was obviously *bona fide*. And yet I had the feeling that he hadn't told me the whole truth, that he was holding something back. I wondered, too, where the professor fitted in.

As if guessing my thoughts, Somerville said quietly:

"The captain and I are old friends. And young Ross was my god-son."

"And you've given up your job to help the captain find him?"

I must have sounded skeptical, for the professor smiled. "I've not had to give anything up," he said. "I'm a lecturer at McGill University. In botany. I put in for my sabbatical year."

I thought carefully; then I turned to Ross.

"Hasn't it occurred to you," I said, "that the whaling company might be doing you a kindness by keeping things in the dark?"

"They hinted as much."

"But you still want the truth? However painful?"

The captain nodded.

"I can face pain," he said, "better than uncertainty."

"All right," I said slowly. "I'll tell you about your son. As much as anyone can tell you.

"He was our helicopter pilot aboard the *Northern Harvester*. You know that already, of course. Last September he took off on a routine flight to spot for whales. But instead of heading south into the area he'd been ordered to search, he headed north-west; in a dead straight line. There was nothing wrong with his helicopter, but he didn't turn back. There was nothing wrong with his radio, but he didn't answer our calls. He went on heading north-west; and he was never seen or heard of again. Two things are certain. First: the whole affair was premeditated. In other

18

words, sir, to put it bluntly, your son stole the helicopter. Second: I'm afraid he can't have survived. The area he flew into is the bleakest part of the Arctic; three-quarters of a million square miles of uninhabited pack-ice that isn't even properly mapped. I'm sorry" I added, "that I can't give you better news."

I had quite expected the captain to take me up on the point of the helicopter being stolen; but instead he went off on another tack, coming straight out with one question I didn't want to answer.

"Have you any idea," he said, "why he did it?"

"Several people," I said slowly, "have theories."

"And what is your theory?"

I walked across to a porthole and knocked the ashes out of my pipe. I still hadn't quite decided how much to tell the captain, and I needed a few extra seconds to make up my mind. By the time the burning tobacco had hit the sea, I had come to a decision. Right or wrong, I wouldn't do things by halves.

"I think," I said, "that your son went to search for the graveyard of the whales."

"The graveyard of the whales!" exclaimed the captain. "Where on earth is that?"

"That," I said, "is something I don't like to talk about in a ship's lounge—even if it is apparently deserted."

The captain looked at me curiously.

"Mr. Rogers," he said, "everything about my son's disappearance seems to be highly mysterious. Would you be willing to come across to my cabin? You could tell us about this graveyard of the whales in privacy there?"

Well, I agreed. I could, quite justifiably, have refused; but I decided, on the spur of the moment, to help Captain Ross as much as I could. Looking back, I am amazed to think what an incredible chain of events stemmed from that apparently harmless decision.

2

The Graveyard of the Whales

ROSS'S CABIN was on the main deck immediately below the bridge; and a very fine cabin it was. It had been two cabins originally, but these had been knocked into one a couple of years ago to accommodate Sir Ian Kinross (of Kinross and Jameson) when he had come north to visit his refinery at Pangnirtung. In the sitting recess which led off from the sleeping quarters there was a small sofa and a pair of easy chairs, and these we now drew up to form a semicircle round the electric wall-fire—of which we were very thankful, since the night was cold and the *Dunvegan*'s air-conditioning none too effective. As soon as the three of us were comfortably settled the captain looked at me expectantly.

"Now, sir," he said, "perhaps you'll tell us about this graveyard of the whales? And what makes you think my son went to search for it?"

I stretched my hands to the fire, spreading my fingers to its warmth.

"It's a queer story," I said, "and before I start I'd like you to promise something. That you won't pass on anything I tell you without my permission. Do you agree to that?"

The captain nodded, and Somerville raised his hand.
"I swear," he said.

I settled back in my chair. "Well," I began, "as you probably know, whales have been hunted for a good many thousand years, but there are still a lot of things that aren't known about them. Elementary things: like what they drink,[1] how they mate, and what happens to them when they die. In this last respect, whales are like elephants, you know; you hardly ever find one that's died from natural causes. And that, I've no doubt, is why the story grew up that both animals go to a special graveyard to die—the elephants to some sort of clearing in the heart of the jungle, the whales to the shore of some lonely undiscovered island. In the old days of whaling this story was pretty widely believed. Special expeditions were fitted out to search for the graveyard. But it was never found. And gradually the story of it became turned into a sort of old wives' tale: a fo'c'sle yarn spun on winter evenings: a pipe dream, like the Eldorado of the men of the Klondike. Then—let me think now, it must be seventy or eighty years ago—the legend took on a new lease of life. For when the San Francisco whalers came up through the Bering Strait and started to work the Arctic coast round the mouth of the Mackenzie, they found that the Eskimo in those parts also had a legend about the graveyard of the whales.

"Now I needn't bother you with the details of this legend, but the gist of it goes like this. According to Eskimo folklore, many thousands of years ago the whale tribe were guilty of some specially terrible crime—eating the other animals' young, I think it was—and as a punishment the gods decreed that henceforth all whales were cursed; in life their mouths were to be sealed up,[2] and in death they were to be barred from entering heaven and their bodies were to drift for ever round the underground waters of hell. And it is because of this decree—according to the Eskimoes—that when a whale gets old it goes to a special

[1] The scientists say that whales do not drink sea-water; this is proved by the fact that their body fluids are non-saline, they never sweat salt, nor have they any device for evaporating it. K. R.

[2] This, according to the Eskimos, accounts for the baleen grid at the back of a whale's mouth. Kipling, as readers of the *Just So Stories* will recall, had another explanation for it. K. R.

graveyard at the mouth of hell—so that its body is all ready and waiting to be tipped straight down to the underworld the moment it dies.

"Well, the tie-up is obvious, isn't it? Find the mouth of the Eskimo hell and you find the graveyard. It sounded easy; but there turned out to be a snag—and a pretty insuperable one. None of the Eskimoes knew where the mouth of hell was—or if they did know, they were all too scared of the place to let on. On the strength of various rumours, a number of expeditions were fitted out; but none of them found anything; one vanished without trace, and another got itself stuck in the pack ice. This damped down enthusiasm. And gradually, as the years passed and more and more of the Arctic became opened up and no graveyard was found, the legend became discredited: became more of an old wives' tale than ever.

"And that's been the position for years now. The legend of the graveyard is something that every whaler knows, but none believes in. Everything about it, you see, is so indefinite. Nobody has ever got hold of anything concrete. Nobody, that is"—I turned to Captain Ross—"except your son."

The others had been listening quietly all this time; the professor taking notes in shorthand, the captain staring straight through me.

"And just what," the latter asked, "did my son get hold of?"

"If only I knew!" I said. "If I could answer that, I wouldn't be here now. I'd be looking for the graveyard myself. But perhaps the best thing I can do is to describe the events that led up to your son's disappearance."

The captain nodded eagerly.

"It's an inconclusive sort of story," I warned him. "Rather like a jigsaw puzzle with the key-piece missing. But I'll make it as clear as I can.

"Looking back, I can see it all started with an electric storm. The *Harvester* was west of Baffin Bay at the time, and young Ross was up in his helicopter on a routine search, when the cloud banks blew up, unexpected and against the wind. To cut a long story short, your son got into difficulty, ran for shelter and crash-landed close to a Company post on the tip of Somerset Island. He spent the best part of a week at the post, repairing the helicopter and waiting for the storm to blow itself out. And while he waited, something pretty peculiar must have happened. For when he got back aboard the *Harvester* he was a changed man. He was completely preoccupied: so much so that his ordinary work and the ordinary everyday things of life no longer interested him. We tried to make him snap out of it: tried to get him to tell us what had happened. But even I, who knew him better than most" (I noticed the captain nodded) "had no luck. He had a secret. He wasn't going to share it. And that was that.

"Well, it was the middle of the whaling season. Aboard the *Harvester* we were working fourteen hours a day: were far too busy in other words to lose any sleep over a mysterious helicopter pilot. We soon stopped trying to pump him. The result was—as any psychologist would have prophesied—that in due course he came to confide in us! Or rather, in me."

The captain leaned forward eagerly.

"One night," I said, "your son invited me down to his cabin, opened up a bottle of rum and said—quite casually —'What would you do, Keith, if you'd discovered the graveyard of the whales?'

"So that's it, I thought! And I was pretty astonished, I can tell you.

" 'If I was certain I'd found it,' I said, 'I'd sell the location to the whaling company.'

" 'For how much?'

"I remember I thought carefully. The boy was obviously in earnest; he didn't want any smart-Alec answers.

" 'Fifty thousand pounds,' I said at last.

"He burst out laughing at that, and I looked at him curiously.

" 'Have you really found it?' I asked him.

"He nodded.

" 'Where?'

" 'Not for fifty thousand pounds,' he said. 'Not even for five hundred thousand!'

"Now this, I thought, was getting ridiculous; for although the location would certainly be valuable it couldn't possibly, it seemed to me, be worth all that. And I remember I said as much to young Ross. He looked at me very straight—just as you're looking now—and said, 'Hasn't it ever occurred to you, Keith, that the whales in the grave-yard could be literally worth their weight in gold?'

"He wasn't joking. And he hadn't had too much to drink. He meant what he said. Literally. I could only gape at him, disbelievingly, while I tried to work out the value of ninety tons of gold. 'No,' I said at last, 'that *hadn't* occurred to me!'

"He smiled. 'You don't believe me,' he said, 'do you?'

"Well, I was foolish then. Looking back I can see I ought to have given him a clever answer: to have egged him on. But I didn't. I gave him an honest answer.

" 'I'd like to believe you,' I said. 'But common sense says no. Unless you've proof? A single grain of concrete proof?'

"He nodded at that. 'You're right,' he said. 'I'll have to have proof.' I remember he jumped up from his chair and began to pace up and down the cabin. Then, quite suddenly, he seemed to make up his mind. He poured out a couple of tots of rum, pushed one of the glasses across to me, and about the graveyard I couldn't get him to utter another word. He shut up like a clam. I tried to edge the conversation back to whaling, but he wouldn't wear it. I asked straight out what it was he'd discovered, but he shook his head and smiled. I tried to get him tight on his own rum, but he was carefully abstemious. He just wasn't going to talk.

"Two days later he flew off in his helicopter and was never heard of again.

"And that, I'm afraid"—I turned to Captain Ross—"is all I can tell you. As I see it we've got a puzzle with the key-piece missing. Your son flew off to get proof that he'd found the graveyard—I think we're safe in assuming that. But where he went to we haven't a clue."

I had half expected the captain to be disappointed at what I had told him; but he wasn't. Puzzled perhaps, but not disappointed. He got up and started to pace the cabin, and I thought—not for the first time—how closely he resembled his son.

"What's your theory?" he asked me. "Do you think he sighted the graveyard during the storm? Then went back to make certain?"

I shook my head.

"That's possible," I said, "but I don't think it's likely.

You see the country round Baffin Bay—that's where the storm was—has been pretty well explored. The whaling fleets go there every year. The Company trappers have a whole chain of posts. I suppose it's just possible the grave-yard's tucked away in some odd corner. But it's not likely."

"Then what *is* your theory?"

"I don't believe," I said slowly, "that Donald Ross ac-. tually *saw* the graveyard. I think he picked up some clue as to where it was. Remember that after he crash-landed he spent a week at the Company post on Somerset Island. Now its my belief that while he was there he came across some piece of evidence; evidence which pointed not only to where the dead whales were; but also to their being fab-ulously valuable."

"Have you any idea what this evidence was?"

I shook my head. "None at all," I said.

The captain and professor exchanged glances, and I had, once again, the feeling that they were holding some-thing back. In the slightly awkward silence that followed, the hum of the air-conditioning sounded unusually loud. Then Captain Ross said quietly, "I think I know what evi-dence he found."

I looked at him in astonishment.

"Mr. Rogers," he went on, "a few minutes ago you asked us to promise something: not to pass on what you told us without permission. If I take you into my confi-dence, will you give a similar undertaking?"

I nodded.

He looked at me hard; then, apparently satisfied, he got up, unlocked one of his suitcases and took out a heavily sealed envelope. Carefully slitting the flap he pulled out a letter and a sheet of yellow parchment.

"These," he said, "were found among my son's personal papers. He must have known that if anything happened to him the Company would forward them on, unopened, to his next of kin. Would you read the letter first." And he handed me a single sheet of ship's note-paper.

I recognized the paper at once; it was the *Northern Harvester's*. I looked at the date: September 4th, 1958: the day after young Ross had invited me down to his cabin: the day before he had disappeared. I read the let-ter:

25

My dear Dad,

If you ever read this it will mean that things have gone wrong and I won't be coming back. If this is the case I want to say "thank you" for all the wonderful times we have had together.

The sheet of parchment that comes with this letter is valuable, Dad. It will make you rich as Midas. All you have to do is take it to someone you can trust who knows about whaling. (Somebody like Captain Saulberg or Keith Rogers.)

As you know, I was never much good at writing letters, and I don't know how to end this one except by saying good-bye and good luck and God be with you always.

Donald.

I handed the letter back. Ross was watching me carefully. "Would you like to see the parchment?" he asked.

"Very much," I said. And without a word he handed me the sheet of heavy yellowing paper, its edges acrumble, its writing faded with age.

Now what I expected I can't really say. Some sort of chart, perhaps, with X marks the spot in red ink; or maybe a letter written by some lonely trapper or whaler who'd been hitting the bottle. To be quite frank, I was prepared to be skeptical. Already, it seemed to me, this piece of parchment had sent young Ross to his death. And much as I wanted to believe in the graveyard, I didn't intend to be over-credulous.

I fingered the parchment critically. It certainly looked as old as the hills. But one couldn't be too sure. I didn't read it. I put it face down on the table.

"What's this supposed to be?" I asked.

It was Somerville who answered. "An original page," he said, "torn from a Hudson's Bay Company Diary. Written by the Company Factor in 1672."

"Is it genuine?"

He nodded.

"How do you know?"

"The paper and ink have been analyzed."

"That doesn't make it a genuine Company record," I argued. "It might be a forgery, written say three hundred years ago."

Somerville smiled.

26

"It's genuine all right," he said. "I got the Hudson's Bay Company to radio their post on Somerset Island where Donald landed. They confirmed they'd got original Diaries there. *And* that this particular page from the Diary for 1672 was missing."

My interest quickened. Olde Chartes with pirates' heads and bags of gold in the corner were one thing, a genuine Company record another. I picked up and read the parchment.

It wasn't at all what I had expected.

Sat. October 19th, 1672, (I read). *Spent this morning trimming a caSk, wch work I had juSt completed when Several NativeS approached from the Norward. In General Such are Savage and brutelike, eating fleSh raw and in their cloathing not at alle clene. But theSe wch came now were of fair manner's, and aSkd for foode, wch I gave them after I had aScertained they had Skin's with wch to make payment. With the NativeS was a younge girl, who had yellow hair, and whom I took at firSt for a white woman, for She waS comely and of a moSt bewitchen Sent of FlowerS. But they told me She came from cloSe to the mouth of Hell, from that iSland immediately beyond the Summer Ice off wch the Sun Sets. Her Sent She kepen in a box or whalebone locket about her Arm, and to the otherS She would not Speeke, but pined alle the time for her home, tho none durSt take her back there. In payment for the foode they gave me SkinS which I liSt aS followS:— Arctic Fox 17, Marten 7, UrSuS (white) 2, Arctic Hare 17 . . .*

(The last few words of the last line had been cut away—I assumed for the analysis of paper and ink.)

I read the entry three times. It was a queer story and no mistaking it. I spotted the clue about the mouth of hell at once—that was certainly something. But I had the feeling that there was more to it than that. And the third time of reading, I got it.

I sat suddenly very still. Amazed. Young Ross's words came flooding back to me. . . . "Hasn't it ever occurred to you, Keith," he had said, "that the whales in the graveyard could be literally worth their weight in gold. . . ." And, by God, I thought, if we can believe this parchment, he's right. It was the biggest thing I had ever heard of. I jumped up, knocking over the table and the three glasses of Scotch which Ross had just poured out.

"Ambergris!" I cried.

The others looked at me blankly.

"Don't you see!" I waved the parchment excitedly. "There's ambergris in the graveyard. Get there, and you'll be millionaires."

It wasn't surprising that they didn't know what I was talking about. That was the beauty of the whole set-up. Only a whaler *could* see the connection—the fabulous connection—between parchment and graveyard; that, of course, was why no one else had followed the clue up.

"Steady on" Ross grunted, mopping the whisky off his coat. "What *is* ambergris anyhow?"

"Look," I said, "I'll explain. The parchment tells us two things." I righted the table and smoothed out the tattered piece of paper. "First, it tells us where the graveyard is. Remember the Eskimo legend—that when the whales are about to die they go to the mouth of hell? Well, the parchment tells us where the mouth of hell is. Look: *'She came from clo'se to the mouth of Hell, from that iSland immediately beyond the Summer Ice off wch the Sun SetS.'* Now where's a map?" I waited impatiently while Somerville ferreted out a School Atlas which was the best sort of map we could lay our hands on on the spur of the moment. Then I turned up the Arctic. "Look, there's the line of the Summer Ice. Now we want an island immediately beyond it. And not any island, but the most westerly one—that'll be the one *'off wch the Sun SetS.'* Here it is!" I pointed to an island deep in the North West Territory. "Prince Patrick Island. That's where you'll find the mouth of hell. And the graveyard."

My excitement was infectious. The others crowded round the map.

"Sounds possible," Ross grunted.

"Possible!" I cried, my vows of skepticism quite gone by the board. "It's certain as night follows day. And that's not the end of the story. The graveyard isn't full of any old whales. It's full of one particular species. Sperm whales. And the Sperm whales are full of ambergris. Just think of it; ton after ton of ambergris: worth five guineas an ounce!"

"How do you know?" Somerville's voice was sharp with skepticism. "Explain it simply. Step by step."

"Look at the parchment," I said. "See what the Factor wrote: that the fair-haired Eskimo girl had *'the moSt bewitchen Sent of FlowerS . . . wch She kepen in a box or whalebone locket.'* Now what do you reckon he meant by that?"

"That she had some sort of scent, I guess: some sort of perfume."

"Exactly. He couldn't have meant anything else. And how did she get the perfume?"

They put forward various suggestions, all of which I promptly hit on the head: that she had got it from a white woman—but I pointed out that in 1672 no white woman had ever been anything like as far north as Somerset Island; that she had got it by barter—but I pointed out that those days (and indeed today) perfume was unknown both to Eskimoes and Indians. In the end they hit on the only possible answer.

"I suppose," Somerville said, "she must have made it."

I nodded. "And to make perfume," I said, "you *must* have ambergris. It's the only fixative in the world. Always has been, always will be. That's why it's worth its weight in gold—and more. Now how," I went on, "do you think the girl got ambergris?"

Somerville shook his head. "You tell us," he said.

"You can take it from me," I said, "ambergris is found in one place and one place only: in the stomach of Sperm whales.[1] And not in every Sperm whale either, only in about one in twenty. In other words, the girl must have come from a place where there's a plentiful supply of Sperm whales. Do you agree with that?"

The others nodded. It was the only possible conclusion.

[1] For those with inquiring minds and strong stomachs, ambergris is formed as follows: Most species of whale feed on krill (tiny shrimplike vertebrata less than a quarter of an inch in length); but Sperm whales feed on octopus. And every now and then the hard, indigestible beak of one of these octopuses will lodge in a Sperm's intestines. There it will act as an irritant, to alleviate which the whale secretes a fatty mucus over the offending beak. Thus, in the same way as a pearl is formed inside an oyster, so ambergris is formed inside the whale. Only ambergris is far more valuable than any pearl. It forms in lumps of anything up to a hundred pounds, which are valued at five guineas an ounce. K. R.

"Now the point's this," I went on. "Sperm aren't usually found in the Arctic—I've been whaling off the North West Territories these thirty years, and in all that time, I've come across no more than a couple of Sperm, washed up on the Mackenzie delta. In other words, there'd be no chance, in the ordinary course of events, of the girl coming across a collection of dead Sperm. In the Artic there's only one place where Sperm *could* be found in large numbers. And that's in the graveyard. On the shore of Prince Patrick Island."

For several minutes we sat in silence, looking at the parchment, thinking things over, while the old *Dunvegan* lurched uneasily through the swell. Then, carefully and methodically, we went over the facts, testing the strength of every link in our chain of evidence. And every link held—right from the genuineness of the original parchment down to the final conclusion we could draw from the Factor's entry. There was no doubt about it: we had unearthed the secret of the graveyard of the whales. And what a fabulous secret it was!

I turned to Ross. "Your son will have flown to Prince Patrick Island," I said, "to get a sample of ambergris as proof."

He nodded, and I could see a seed of hope beginning to take root.

"I'm very much afraid," I added gently, "there's no hope of his still being alive. No man could survive a week in that part of the Arctic, let alone a year."

The captain jumped up at that and began to pace the cabin. "Mr. Rogers," he burst out, "I'm not convinced that my son is dead: not convinced at all. I'm going to look for him. I'm going to follow his trail to Prince Patrick Island, and, if need be, beyond. And I'll not give up till I find him, or till I've certain proof he is dead. Now, sir! Will you come with me?"

I was quite taken aback at this.

"I'd want time," I said slowly, "to think that over. My first reaction is that I'm far too old for such a wild-goose chase."

Both Ross and Somerville looked disappointed.

"Mr. Rogers," the former said, "my friend and I don't know the Arctic. You do: no man better. Your help would be invaluable. If you'll agree to join forces you can

30

pretty well make what conditions you like—and, of course, I'd pay you well."

It was a generous proposal: certainly not the sort to be sneezed at by a poor whaler and trapper. Yet for some reason I still held back—perhaps I had a premonition of things to come.

"Your offer's very tempting," I said. "But I must have time to think it over. I'll give you an answer by the time we get to Pangnirtung."

And so we left it; and I said good night to the others and made my way to my cabin along the *Dunvegan*'s swaying corridors, and fell asleep to dream of ambergris and fair-haired Eskimoes and the legendary graveyard of the whales.

3

An Expedition Is Formed

THE *Dunvegan* takes ten days to cover the seven hundred miles from Hamilton Inlet to Pangnirtung, for she puts in at a fair number of landing stages *en route;* besides, she is a decrepit old vessel and seldom works up to more than eight or nine knots. But for me at any rate, the voyage always passes far too quickly; for the splendid desolation of the Labrador and Baffin Island coastline never fails to delight me: mile after hundred mile of majestic cliffs, fringed by snow-white isles, with the wide rip flowing darkly between like ink spilt into the sea. It is a coast which makes one conscious of the grandeur of nature and the littleness of man, and I can't help feeling that a voyage along it would do a power of good to all the self-important business men who spend their lives in cities making money. But that is by the way.

All the time we were heading north I was, of course, thinking over Ross's offer—and the more I thought of it the better I liked it. We didn't, by tacit agreement, talk any more of the graveyard; but I spent a good deal of time with the captain and professor and I came to the conclusion that if the three of us did team up we should get on well together—and that, believe me, is pretty important in a venture such as ours. Also, being a cautious man, I made inquiries into the captain's financial status. He was, I discovered, more than comfortably off, being one of those fortunate people with inherited investments and modest needs.

After ten days we duly fetched up at Pangnirtung, the old whaling station at the foot of Cumberland Sound. It is a beautiful place—though the smell of boiling blubber from the refinery rather takes the gilt off the gingerbread —and after dinner the three of us went up to the boat deck to enjoy the view. The *Dunvegan* by this time was swinging at her anchor beside the bar, a crescent moon was rising over the hills, the stars were gemlike, and the water was motionless and black as shale; it was a scene of tranquil beauty such as one meets with only occasionally in out-of-the-way corners of the world.

"Well, Rogers," the captain said presently, as we stood together enjoying the view, "I very much hope you'll be coming with us to look for my son."

I walked across to the deck-rail, knocked out my pipe and watched the tobacco fall with a little hiss into the sea. I was in a difficult position. The whole affair intrigued me; I had to admit that. But on the other hand, the last thing I wanted was to be in any way responsible for a pair of greenhorns like Ross and Somerville embarking on a quest which—to say the least—was likely to be fraught with difficulty and danger.

"Captain Ross," I said slowly, "I don't think you quite realize what a job you're taking on. Prince Patrick Island lies in the heart of the Arctic: slap in the middle of three-quarters of a million square miles of ice that hasn't even been properly mapped. Just think of it. No food: no vegetation: no Eskimoes: simply a solid sheet of ice. Just to get to Prince Patrick Island would be a major undertaking. But you haven't only to get to the island, you have to search it as well. Imagine combing an island the size of Scotland, swept by blizzards, in a temperature of minus forty. That's no job for amateurs." I paused. "I warn you quite bluntly, if you go it alone I don't think much of your chances of coming back. What happened to your son will happen to you. So take my advice, gentlemen. Go to Kinross and Jameson. Put your cards on the table and ask them to fit out an expedition. Believe me, once they hear your story they'll be as keen as you to get to the grave-yard."

The captain gestured impatiently. "I don't care a fig for the graveyard," he said. "I want to find my son."

"I'm sorry," I said quietly, "but you must face the facts. There's not one chance in a thousand he's still alive."

He shrugged. "A chance is a chance, whatever the odds. My friend and I are quite determined to go through with this. Eh, Somerville?"

The professor nodded.

I could see that they meant it. No matter what I did or said, they were going to search for the graveyard. And there was no holding them back.

Well, as I have said, the whole affair intrigued me—the thought of all that ambergris lying unclaimed fairly made my mouth water; and I knew now that I need never re-proach myself for having led the others into danger—they would have got themselves there in any case.

"Strikes me," I said, "that the pair of you are set on committing suicide. And if that's the case I might as well come along too. With someone who knows the Arctic you may live a few days longer!"

Somerville's face lit up, and Ross thumped me heartily on the back. "Good for you," he cried. And on the profes-sor's suggestion we adjourned below to drink to our expe-dition's success.

Next morning we went ashore. I fixed us up with rooms in the Grenfell Mission—where the doctor is an old friend of mine—and here we got down to business, in far more privacy than we would have enjoyed in the local hotel.

First, we agreed on terms: Ross to pay all expenses, I to get £100 a month for as long as the search was contin-ued, and any proceeds to be divided equally between the three of us. We then drew up plans. And here we had a stroke of luck. For it turned out that Ross was an ex-Fleet Air Arm pilot (I gathered that before the war he had taken part in flying displays at Hendon, doing odd things like looping-the-loop while chained to another aircraft), and he felt quite confident of being able to fly us to Prince Patrick Island. This, of course, both saved us an arduous trek and, at the same time, simplified the problem of sur-veying the island once we had reached it. All the same, aircraft are fallible things—especially in a temperature of minus forty—and we obviously needed a second string to our bow. We therefore hit on the following arrangement: that we would buy a plane, load up with stores at Pangnirtung, and fly as far as the Parry Islands—the nearest inhabited region to Prince Patrick island; here we would land, buy dogs and dog meat at one of the northern Eskimo settlements, and then fly the final stretch to the island with the dogs aboard. Once arrived, we would survey as much of Prince Patrick Island as we could by air and the rest by sledge.

Now I needn't weary you with the details of all these arrangements: the buying of the plane (an amphibious Sea Otter); the stocking up with equipment and stores (a lot of which had to be specially flown in from Quebec) and the hundred-and-one delays we had to endure and the thousand-and-one difficulties we had to iron out. Enough to say that for five solid weeks we were planning, preparing and testing (Ross chiefly concerned with the plane, I with stores, and Somerville—for some reason best known to himself—with a strange selection of maps and reports from the local library). Then at last we were ready to go.

July 18 was the day of our departure, and soon after sunrise—early as it was—the pastor from the Grenfell Mission came down to the airstrip, at Ross's request, to give us his blessing. It was a moving little ceremony: the wind tugging the pastor's surplice, the sun turning the snow-covered tarmac to gold, and the words "Preserve us, O Lord, from the dangers of sea and storm" taking on a special sort of significance. For ours was a strange quest; there was no telling where it would lead us, and I for one had more than a few doubts as to whether we'd come out of it alive.

The others, I think, must have felt much as I did; for as the Sea Otter slid for the last time into Cumberland Sound, we were all unusually subdued. We taxied across to the refinery in silence. Then we swung into the wind; Ross revved up the engine; the Sea Otter surged forward in a slipstream of spray; the spray thickened; the aircraft bucketed slightly; then we lifted clear of the water. Our search was under way.

We circled Pangnirtung three times, gaining height; then

we set course for the Parry Islands: over a thousand miles distant, in the heart of the Arctic. I hoped that Captain Ross was a good navigator.

I append a detailed list of the equipment and stores we took with us in the Sea Otter. I make no apology for giving this in full, for good and well-chosen equipment is of vital importance to any expedition. And as it turned out more than one of the items listed below saved our lives.

1. One 16-inch sledge of laminated yew. A béautifully constructed piece of work, being very strong, very light and perfectly balanced. It was not completely new, having been used once for an oil survey; but in my opinion was all the better for that, since I could check that the wood was well seasoned; also any faults in a sledge usually show out on the first trip.
2. One set of leather dog-harness. (The dogs themselves, you remember, we hoped to pick up on the fringe of the Parry Islands.)
3. Three sets of skis (plus spares).
4. Three sets of snowshoes (plus spares).
5. Three sets of Alpine climbing equipment (boots, ice-axes, crampons, pitons, goggles and rope).
6. Three complete changes of clothing apiece.
7. One *de luxe* Meade-type tent. This was a larger version of the type used by Everest expeditions. It was made of Willesden canvas (which is wind and waterproof) and was book-like in shape with inverted V supports at either end. It was large enough to sleep the three of us in comfort and weighed only a shade over 40 lb. (47 lb. to be exact, including guy-ropes and aluminum tent pegs).
8. Three spongy-rubber ground sheets.
9. Three Jaeger sleeping bags. These were made of wool-fleece and eiderdown and were wonderfully warm and light, weighing only 8¾ lb. apiece.
10. Nine Hudson Bay Point-type blankets.
11. One set of aluminum cooking utensils.
12. One Primus cooking stove (plus fuel).
13. One mincer (for caribou, which we expected to be our staple diet, are stringy beasts, tough enough to

test the teeth of a Mastodon and the digestion of an ostrich).

14. Three chests of assorted food-stuffs. These contained all the usual ingredients—flour, tea, sugar, condensed milk, cocoa, raisins, chocolate, tinned meat, butter, etc.—plus a few special items which experience had taught me would come in useful: lemon juice, for example; curry powder (which can turn the toughest caribou into an appetizing stew) and arrowroot (very good for those with upset stomachs —which, by the way, are all too frequent when the only supply of water is melted ice).

15. One set of traps, for small game such as marten and hare.

16. Two large bags of mixed gifts for trading (these contained all the usual bric-à-brac: beads, scented soap, cheap knives, etc.).

17. One medicine chest, containing everything from Elastoplasts to morphia and tourniquets.

18. Two dozen sticks of dynamite: useful for breaking ice or stunning fish.

19. One set of complete navigational equipment, and as many maps of the Parry Islands and Prince Patrick Island as we could lay our hands on.

And finally, fire-arms. After much discussion and no little leg-pulling on the part of the others, we agreed on the following:

20. Three Lee-Enfield ex-service .303s. Rather old-fashioned weapons, but very reliable, and a type we were all accustomed to using. Good for shooting wolves, medium-sized game such as caribou, or, of course, men.

21. Two twelve-bore shot guns: excellent for small game and birds for the pot.

22. Two Sten guns. These were my idea; they caused the others a good deal of amusement; but there is never any harm, in my opinion, in being prepared for the worst.

4

Flight North

I DON'T intend to relate all the details of our flight to the
Parry Islands, a journey which would have taken us a couple of months by sledge, but which we accomplished by
plane in just over a week. Our adventures *en route* were
many and various; but they were the sort of adventures
which befall all Arctic fliers (engine-trouble, blizzards and
the prevalence, far into the day, of ground mist) and with
one exception—which I shall come to in a moment—I see
no point in setting them down at length. Enough to say
that we flew the breadth of Baffin Island, crossed the tip of
Lancaster Sound (where just over a year ago young Ross
had disappeared) and finally fetched up at the airstrip on
Cape Farewell—the most northerly landing stage in the
world, specially built for planes supplying the D.E.W. Line
radar posts. Here we refuelled to capacity (including the
filling of our special 500-gallon reserve tanks), knowing
that ahead of us lay nothing but a scattering of Eskimo
villages. Then we flew on, probing ever deeper into the
heart of the Arctic, until at last we came to the fringe of
the Parry Islands.

It was here that there occurred the one incident I am
going to narrate in detail: and a hair-raising incident it

was, which very nearly halted our expedition before it had got fairly under way.

We had landed as usual at midday, on the edge of a frozen lake, and were about to embark on our customary afternoon routine; that is to say, Ross was preparing to set to work on servicing the Sea Otter—a job which invariably took him at least four hours a day, while Somerville and I were getting ready to go hunting—which we did each afternoon so as to conserve our stores. As we were strapping on our snowshoes I could see the captain through the Perspex of the Sea Otter cockpit, collecting together his servicing tools.

"Can you toss out the rifles?" I shouted up to him.

He slid back the cockpit window and passed out our two Lee-Enfields.

"And yours," I suggested.

A pause, and the third rifle followed the others.

"I'll stack yours against the tailplane," I called up.

He nodded. I could see he was only half listening; his mind was on his coming airframe inspection. But after all, I thought, what does it matter? He won't need the rifle anyhow. So Somerville and I left him tinkering about with his spanners and grease-nipples, while we set off along the shore of the lake. We were after walrus; but, as it turned out, we ran into something very different.

Less than half a mile from the plane we came to tracks: the tracks of a bear, so fresh that the snow around the edges was still acrumble. I could tell by the bristle marks that the tracks were made by a polar bear, the most unpredictable of the bear family (all of whom, by the way, are especially dangerous in the early autumn when they are getting ready to hibernate). We should have turned back. I knew it at the time. But Somerville, who in the last few days had been shooting walrus, fox and caribou with all the aplomb of a veteran woodsman, was eager for fresh worlds to conquer. "Let's track it," he whispered. "A bear would keep us in meat for weeks!"

And, foolishly and against my better judgment, I agreed. We slipped off our safety catches, and, guns at the ready, began to follow the footprints towards the lake.

The ground wasn't easy. It was a mass of snow-covered boulders, many of which were much the size of a man— or of a bear. I went first, with one eye on the snow, the

39

other on the boulders, one of which I expected any second to leap up with an angry roar. Somerville followed, five yards behind. It was some consolation to know he was a good shot. But not much. The Arctic sun streamed down. It was near heatless. But I was soon damp with sweat. For what seemed like hours but was in fact probably less than ten minutes, we picked our way cautiously towards the lake. When we reached it we saw, to our great relief, that the tracks left the land and headed out across the ice. We followed eagerly. In the open we could move faster and far more freely, and for a while we made good progress, expecting any moment to sight our quarry lumbering across the frozen water. But there soon came a development I didn't like. Quite suddenly the tracks altered course; they doubled back and headed straight for the shore—straight for the bay where we had left Ross and the Sea Otter. Somerville and I looked at each other uneasily. We quickened our step.

As we neared the bay we could hear the noise of hammering and the cheerful baritone of Captain Ross—who nearly always broke into song when his inspections were going well. The words came to us clearly, strangely incongruous in the stillness of the Arctic: "Oh, my darling, oh my darling, oh my darling Clementine, Thou art lost and gone for—"

The hammering stopped. The last line was cut abruptly off.

"Come on," I shouted. "Quick!"

We rushed forward, and rounding the headland were brought up short by a sight which pricked up my hair like the quills of a porcupine. Ross was standing on a pair of steps alongside the Sea Otter's wing. In his hand was a small oily rag; his rifle still leaned against the tailplane—well out of reach; and sniffing at the bottom rung of the steps was the most enormous polar bear I have even seen.

It was a full hundred yards from headland to bear. The sun was straight in our eyes, and Ross was dangerously close to the line of fire. Instinctively we brought up our rifles. Then we hesitated.

"Wait," I hissed. "See if he moves."

And move the bear did—though not in the way I had hoped. For several seconds he snuffled round the foot of the steps. Then he reared suddenly up. His paws weaved to and fro in front of his face. And he lunged straight at the captain.

Two rifles cracked simultaneously. The bear grunted and clutched at his stomach. And Ross, seizing his opportunity, leaped at the strut connecting the Sea Otter's wings, and swung himself like a trapeze artist onto the upper mainplane. The bear, coughing angrily, scrabbled after him; its claws flayed at the wing, shredding away great ribbons of fabric. We fired again and the bear went reeling against the float. Again, and he careered into the undercarriage which collapsed, with a horrible crash, causing the plane to heel over like a dismasted ship. It needed a full half-dozen shots before the great creature sank to its knees, rolled over and at last lay still.

As we came rushing up. Ross scrambled off the Sea Otter's wing.

"You all right?" Somerville panted.

He nodded.

"*I'm* all right. But the plane isn't."

Ruefully we inspected the damage. Our hearts sank. The starboard wing was a thing of shreds and patches. Great chunks had been clawed off the leading edge; the wingtip had been bent up; the float had disintegrated; and, worst of all, the undercarriage had collapsed, so that the whole plane lay canted over, half-buried in the snow like some derelict hulk in the mud of a silted estuary. I had always thought of air-craft as delicate things; and the damage, it seemed to me, was surely irreparable. But Ross thought otherwise.

"I won't be easy," he said. "but we can patch her up."

And that evening we set to work.

It took us five days, working well into the short Arctic nights, to repair the Sea Otter; five days of heating Bostik that refused to come to the boil; of stretching fabric that wouldn't, in the intense cold, tauten without splitting; and of painting-on dope that solidified to ice before it had left our brushes. It was cold, exhausting, heart-breaking work. Once I leaned too heavily on a soldered strut and it cracked; once a jack slipped, and the landing skid we had spent six hours fashioning was crushed like an eggshell. But Ross didn't let us give up. He kept us at it hour after hour, day after day; until at last the Sea Otter was back on an even keel. Then came the moment all our work had

41

been leading up to: the test flight. Somerville and I watched anxiously from the shore while Ross taxied across the ice. As the plane lifted into the air, I had visions of the whole wing disintegrating. But nothing happened. She flew normally. She landed safely. And next morning saw us again heading north by west, with the Sea Otter, to all outward appearances, none the worse for her buffeting. We had, it seemed, been lucky.

As we probed deeper into the Arctic, the country became increasingly appealing—at least, it struck me as being appealing; the others, I think, considered it somewhat desolate. Certainly it was far from beautiful in the conventional sense; it was too featureless and colorless for that. But it had serenity: a quiet innocence of virgin drifts and sleeping floes, shot with occasional caverns of turquoise and emerald where the ice fell sheer, often hundreds of feet, to the water below. Soon we were well into the Parry Islands: a far-flung scattering of Proterozoic rocks lodged in the Arctic pack ice like so many stones tossed into a sea of cement. It was hard to tell from the air where the islands began and the sea-ice ended, for both were enveloped in a heavy mantel of snow.

On our eleventh day out from Pangnirtung we landed on Bathurst Island—roughly in the center of the archipelago—and as we touched down the Sea Otter gave a queer uncertain lurch. Ross spent the afternoon, the evening and most of the night inspecting the undercarriage. I could tell that he was none too happy, and I guessed he was afraid that part of the landing mechanism had been strained. He jacked the Sea Otter up, and spent five hours raising and lowering her skids. At the end of it all he seemed only half satisfied. He hadn't, I gathered, found anything wrong: but on the other hand, he lacked the facilities for carrying out the sort of inspection that was one hundred per cent conclusive. We would have to be careful, he told us. From now on he would, whenever possible, land on ice rather than snow (i.e, touch-down hull first rather than skid first).

And that, for the next forty-eight hours, was just what we did, landing each afternoon on the sea-ice and then taxi-ing ashore for the night. We were eight hundred miles inside the Arctic Circle by this time, and approaching the last of the Parry Islands. This was the bleakest and most desolate corner of the North West Territories: a wilderness of pack-ice and snow-blanketed island, where maps were only approximate, and the position of the few Eskimo settlements was largely guesswork—for apart from anything else the tribes were nomadic, following the whale and caribou herds in their seasonal migrations. I did, however, know of one settlement which had a degree of permanence. On the east coast of Melville Island (the island next to Prince Patrick Island) the Company had a trading post, and I knew that round it a small village had taken root: a collection of some hundred Eskimoes eking out a precarious existence on the roof of the world. Here, we agreed, was the obvious place to buy dogs.

So it was that just a fortnight after leaving Pangnirtung we were flying along the coast of Melville Island searching for Winter Harbour—the Eskimo settlement. It was a clear morning, with visibility close on fifty miles, and we expected little difficulty in finding the village.

Sure enough it soon came in sight: a cluster of reed huts, sod houses and igloos, scattered along the shore of an ice-choked bay. We came down low, looking for somewhere to land, while the Eskimoes (who had never seen a plane in their lives) ran hither and thither in obvious panic. Had there been anywhere for them to hide they would surely have hidden; as it was, after much scurrying about they disappeared, ostrich-like, into their huts.

"Don't like the look of the ice!" Ross's voice was worried.

I had been so busy watching the Eskimoes that I hadn't given a thought to the ice. But now, looking down, I felt a stab of anxiety. Along the shore the ice pack was broken up into house-sized blocks, jambed tight by drift, and serrated like the teeth of a saw.

"Looks better inland." Somerville pointed towards a miniature plateau about half a mile from the village.

We flew across to it.

The plateau certainly looked as smooth as a billiard table, and the snow, as far as we could judge, was in good condition. We did a couple of dummy runs; then Ross lowered the skids.

"We'll risk it," he grunted. "Safety belts on."

We came in slowly, carefully, in a long shallow approach. Our skids brushed the snow smoothly, softly, with scarcely a jar. For forty or fifty yards the Sea Otter ran straight, gradually losing way. Then it happened. Our starboard skid hit a patch of softness: a drift of powder snow, loose-packed and treacherous. The plane slewed sideways; and before Ross had a chance to correct, the undercarriage, already strained, collapsed.

There was a tilting and slithering; a churning-up of snow; a sickening crunch, and the plane slewed on to her side. For a second everything was noise and grating and jolting and a great darkness of snow pouring in through the shattered cockpit. I remember Ross snapping off the ignition switches. I remember his warning shout.

"Cover your heads!"

Then something struck me a great blow on the back of the neck. And the rest was silence.

5

Into the Unknown

I COULD have been unconscious for only a few seconds, for when I came to snow was still pouring in through the Perspex roof of the cockpit, and Ross was tearing at my safety belt.

"Give us a hand with him"—his voice sounded strangely distant—"Quick. In case the petrol catches."

And I felt myself being half-dragged, half-carried out of the shattered plane. Once in the open my head cleared, and I sat up, blinking.

"You all right?" Somerville's voice was anxious.

I felt the back of my head. "I'm still in one piece," I said.

"Can't say as much," muttered Ross, "for the plane."

We sat in the snow and looked at the wreck of the Sea Otter. I could tell that this time there'd be no patching her up—at least, not with the equipment we had—for her under-carriage had collapsed and her starboard wing had been wrenched off and was splintered as broken glass. She had flown us to the Parry Islands, but she would fly us no farther; that was obvious. They say it's no good crying over spilt milk, but I must admit I could have wept!

We were still inspecting the damage when a man came skiing towards us from the direction of the village. He turned out to be the Factor, a small black-bearded fellow, who, once he had satisfied himself that we weren't fur thieves out to rob his store, did everything possible to help.

Within a couple of hours of the crash we were sitting down in his cabin to a stew of piping-hot walrus heart, while a chain of Eskimoes were unloading our stores from the wrecked plane and stacking them at the back of the hut. When we had eaten our fill, the Factor, who had been watching us closely, turned to me.

"So you're botanists, eh?" He sounded none too credulous.

I nodded; for this was the story we had agreed to stick to.

"Queer time o' year, ain't it, to be startin' an expedition?"

Somerville—thank heavens—was equal to the occasion. In his most professor-like manner he addressed himself to the Factor. "We are here, sir, to study the cycle of growth of *cladonia rangiferina*—reindeer moss, that is. My colleague," he gestured condescendingly at Ross, "believes that even under the snow the moss's growth continues late into the autumn. My own views are somewhat less fanciful . . ." And he proceeded to enlarge on them with a wealth of botanical detail which clearly banished the last of the Factor's doubts as to our *bona fides*. After a while the conversation drifted round to the Sea Otter.

"Now she's bust up, I suppose you'll have to turn back?" The Factor was sympathetic.

This was something we had all been thinking about, but hadn't yet had time to discuss.

"I'm not sure," I said slowly, "that we mightn't push on by sledge."

Somerville looked dubious; but Ross was obviously pleased. "Of course," he said, "we'll push on. Can't be more than a couple of hundred miles to Prince Patrick Island."

"Prince Patrick Island?" The Factor's voice was sharp.

I nodded.

He gave me a strange look. "Why are you headin' for there?"

"Why shouldn't we be?"

He shrugged. "Go where you like. It's no business of mine. But I wouldn't tell the Eskimoes."

Well, I had a splitting headache—the result of cracking my head on the Sea Otter cockpit—and I was in no mood for puzzles or mysteries. While Ross and Somerville checked through the stores and then went off to have a further look at the plane, I dossed down in my sleeping bag. I was tired; but sleep didn't come easily. For some reason I couldn't forget the Factor's warning. And I lay awake hour after hour, my head throbbing, wondering what possible reason there could be for our not telling the Eskimoes that we were bound for Prince Patrick Island.

Next morning we held a council of war. Ross confirmed that we would have to write off the Sea Otter; she needed, he told us, a new mainplane, undercarriage and rudder, her hull was fractured and strained, and the cost of repairing her would be prohibitive. Our stores, on the other hand had suffered surprisingly little. Apart from one already opened food chest, not a thing had been badly damaged. We still, in other words, had enough equipment for a survey and enough food to last us a good three months. And Somerville, the evening before, had ascertained that the Eskimoes would be willing to sell us dogs and dog meat. We got out our maps. It was roughly two hundred miles from Winter Harbour to Prince Patrick Island; less than a fortnight's sledging in good conditions. Once there, I knew there'd be no need to explore the island's interior; for the graveyard (and young Ross, if by some miracle he were still alive) would surely be on the coast, and a circumnavigation, I reckoned, would take us about four to five weeks: the exact time depending on the weather and how closely we had to follow the coastal identations. A fortnight to reach the island, a month to sledge round it, a fortnight to get back . . . and we had food for three months, and could probably squeeze a few further supplies out of the Factor. I looked at the others. Ross, it was obvious, was raring to go. Somerville was doubtful. But the decision, I knew, was up to me.

I pulled out my pipe. While packing the bowl I thought of the Factor's warning. What was it he had said on hearing we were bound for Prince Patrick Island? "Go where you like. But I wouldn't tell the Eskimoes." A strange, unsatis-

47

factory sort of remark. The smoke from my pipe spiraled up, thick and opaque in the still, Arctic air.

"Seems to me," I said slowly, "we don't want to rush a decision on this. If we can get plenty of dogs, plenty of dog meat, and a few extra stores, then I'd say it *might* be okay. But before I'm sure I want to talk to the Factor."

It was late evening before I had the chance of a word with him. All day he had been away on the trap lines; but about nine o'clock the howl of dogs and the cracking of a whip announced his return, and I went across to the store to help him in with his pelts. He'd had a good day: close on a dozen ermine and a couple of fox, one blue, one silver. We carried them into the store hut.

Now a Company store is quite a place. I know of nowhere else on earth—except perhaps an old-fashioned ship's chandler's—so redolent with atmosphere: the white scrubbed beams; the pegged-out wealth of the Arctic—mink, muskrat and ermine, marten and fox, beaver and bear; the tallow and salt; the presses and hone stones, and the wooden packing crates with their archaic lettering, "The Company of Adventurers of England Trading into Hudson's Bay." As we laid out the pelts their tang, saline and at the same time curiously warm, brought a familiar stir of excitement. I could see that the Factor was eager to get on with the skinning.

"Can I give you a hand?"

He looked at me doubtfully; then pushed over hone stone, knife and one of the ermine. For a while we worked in silence, side by side. Out of the corner of my eye I could see him watching me; but he said nothing; not until, a half-hour later, when I passed him the finished skin; then he looked at me, and smiled.

"You're no botanist. You're a trapper."

I laughed. "The other two are botanists. I'm the wet nurse. Seeing they don't catch cold."

He nodded.

"Like we told you last night," I went on, "we're aiming to visit Prince Patrick Island."

His smile died on him. "So?"

"I just hoped you'd tell me something about it."

"Sorry, mister. I never been there."

48

I was surprised. Two hundred miles, to a trapper in the North West Territories, is no more than an average trek.

"Not been there! Why ever not?"

It was some time before he answered; and when he did, his voice was curiously defensive.

"I've got to live with the Eskimoes. No point in upsettin' 'em."

"Upsetting them? They afraid of the island, then?"

"Afraid of it!" He laughed. "They're scared to death of it."

"I wonder," I said slowly, "why."

"Sure I dunno." He began to incise the next of the ermine. "All they say is it's taboo. And that's that."

I had the feeling that he knew more than he was letting on; but I had the feeling, too, that direct questioning would get me nowhere.

"How about reindeer moss?" I asked him. "My friends find any of that on the island?"

"Sure. What else could the caribou eat?" And, seeing my surprise, he went on to explain that early each September a branch of the Alaskan caribou herd passed through Prince Patrick Island on their annual migration to the barrens.

This was news indeed. I questioned the Factor closely. For here—if he had got his facts right—was the safeguard we needed: a supply of food ready and waiting in the event of emergency. Yes, he told me, he had seen the herd himself; yes, it came every year, at much the same time; and yes, there was one particular part of the island it went to—the big valley running inland from the head of Mould Bay.

Having elicited this, I eased up on the questioning, and for a time we worked in silence.

Soon after eleven o'clock the light began to fail. But we went on skinning by the glow of the bulbous oil lamps, slung like great Chinese lanterns between the beams. And after a while another light came stabbing in through the windows: the light of the *aurora borealis,* adance round the curve of the northern horizon. We worked on. And on and on and on.

It was long after midnight by the time the last of the ermine had been skinned and was pegged out ready for salting. The Factor blew out the lamps, padlocked the store, and we walked back to his cabin in silence. I didn't think he was going to mention Prince Patrick Island again; but at the doorway he paused.

"Those two botanists." His voice was gruff. "You want to see they don't catch cold?"

I nodded.

"Then take my advice, mister. There's reindeer moss on Melville Island. Your friends are less likely to catch cold if they do their experiments here."

"But why?"

"I said all I'm going to say. And that's flat. Good night, mister."

And the door closed softly behind him.

Well, I didn't like it. Mysteries always bother me—I suppose because I'm the sort of person who likes to have everything cut and dried. And yet it was obvious we couldn't call off the expedition on account of a single vague and unsubstantiated warning. I undressed slowly; I lay awake a long time, thinking; and in the end I came to the conclusion that I ought to base my decision on nothing but facts. And the facts were these; we had food and equipment for over three months; a survey ought to take less than two months; and in case of emergency we had a stand-by—the migrating herd of caribou.

Next morning we set about disposing of the wreck of the Sea Otter and buying dogs, dog meat and extra stores.

A week later we hit the trail—at dawn on Tuesday, 11 August, to be exact—watched by the entire population of Winter Harbour and a somber, blood-red sun.

"Mush, Queequeg! Mush!"

I sent the twenty-five-foot sealskin whip cracking over the heads of the team and they set off at an exuberant gallop. From that moment we were heading into the unknown.

Now driving huskies is wonderfully exhilarating. I have been doing it on and off for thirty years, but it still gives me a thrill: the hiss of runners over the snow, the long-drawn howl of the dogs (huskies never bark), and the lilt and sway of the sledge: they take one into another world.

50

Neither Ross nor Somerville had done much sledging before, but they were good skiers, and that is half the battle. So all that first day I took them, turn and turn about, on the steering bar, showing them how to manipulate it with one hand while skiing behind and a little to one side of the runners. They did pretty well, too, except when Ross got over-confident and thought he'd try cracking the whip. He cracked it all right; but a twenty-five foot sealskin whip needs an experienced hand, and all he managed to hit was the back of his own head! After that he stuck to the *illi, illi* (for swing left), the *yu, yu* (for swing right), and the long-drawn soothing *ai-ee-ee* for stop. And that, together with strong wrists and common sense, is about all a husky driver needs. We covered twenty-four miles that first day: good going for an inexperienced team of twelve over none too easy country; and eight o'clock in the evening found us dossed-down in our Meade tent, with a snow wall built to windward, and the dogs fed and curled up asleep in the snow. It went against the grain to settle down for the night with the sun still high in the sky; but I knew the danger of rushing things. And by nine o'clock we were as fast asleep as the dogs.

And that first day set the pattern for several days to come. The weather stayed fine, the ice held good, the dogs buckled-to with a will, and in less than a week we had sledged the width of Melville Island (some hundred and sixty miles). The journey wasn't difficult, but it was unbelievably monotonous. For day after day we moved through a virgin wilderness, unrelieved by tree or plant or moss, by bird or animal or fish; for all the sign there was of life we might have been crossing the face of the moon.

Then, late on our sixth day out from Winter Harbour, we came to the sea: to the forty-mile stretch of frozen water which was all that now divided us from our goal.

That evening, while Somerville pitched camp and fed the dogs (a job we did turn and turn about), Ross and I walked down to the shore and looked out across the ice. Was it our imagination or was there, on the north-west horizon, a smudge of darkness: our first glimpse of the mysterious Prince Patrick Island: the island whose secrets (God willing) we would soon be laying bare? We stared eagerly across the wilderness of ice, shading our eyes against the glare of the low-slung sun.

Our contemplation was broken by an excited shout. "Hey! Look what I've found!"

Somerville was waving what appeared to be a tattered envelope. We hurried back.

He had, he told us, found it wedged between a couple of slabs of dog meat. When he had cut the meat, before throwing it to the dogs, the envelope had tumbled out. How it had got there we couldn't imagine. We peered at it in astonishment, passing it from one to another.

"Mr. K. Rogers," the captain read out. "It's addressed to you, Keith. Open it up."

I took the envelope and carefully slit through the flap. What I expected to find I'm none too sure, but certainly not the single sheet of Company note-paper with its five lines of spidery handwriting.

"It's from the Factor at Winter Harbour," I said.

If you are going to Prince Patrick Island, look out for the men with yellow hair.

Dominic Clunnes.

P.S.—Don't come back to ask for explanations because I'm not able to give any.

I passed the note to the others. For several minutes we looked at it in silence, too astonished to speak. Then Somerville helped himself to snuff.

"Mr. Dominic Clunnes," he observed drily, "has a taste for the melodramatic."

I shook my head. My doubts and half-formed fears came flooding back. "Struck me," I said, "he was a level-headed sort of chap. Factors usually are. I think we ought to take this seriously."

Ross was staring hard at the north-western horizon; his eyes, I noticed, were curiously bright. "That island must be quite overcrowded," he said. "Whales. Caribou. Men with yellow hair. And—God grant it—my son."

We stood in a little cluster staring at the smudge on the horizon. For a few seconds, bathed in the rays of the dying sun, it seemed to take on a definite outline: a crouching mass of darkness, enigmatic and vaguely menacing. Then, as the sun set, the outline faded, submerged in the grey uncertain twilight.

"Let's get a good night's sleep," I said. "Tomorrow we'll be there."

6

"We're Being Watched"

NEXT MORNING we struck camp early. The weather was
fine, the ice was good, and we made rapid progress. By
midday Prince Patrick Island had taken on definite shape:
a low featureless littoral sprawled across the northern horizon. The dogs seemed to catch our sense of expectancy,
for the sledge fairly surged forward and by four o'clock
we were nearing land.

From the ice Prince Patrick Island looked reassuringly
normal. Perhaps the cliffs lining the shore were a little
more sheer than usual, the silence a little more absolute,
the whiteness of the snow a little more intense; but these
were differences in degree rather than kind. All the same,
I was taking no chances.

"Ai-ee-ee!"

Fifty yards short of the cliffs I brought the dogs to a
halt. I beckoned to the others. (I ought perhaps to explain
here that when we left Winter Harbour Ross had asked
me to act as expedition leader; it is always as well to have
one person giving the orders, and I had more experience
of the Arctic than either he or Somerville.) "Once we get
ashore," I said, "we'd best keep our eyes skinned. And
keep together."

What sort of trouble I thought we were going to run

into I can't exactly say; but then I'm congenitally cautious, and have always preferred being safe to sorry. We therefore sledged up to Prince Patrick Island with due solemnity and with all the care of a reconnaissance patrol approaching an enemy strongpoint.

Then came the anticlimax. We found we couldn't get ashore!

For several hours we sledged along the foot of the cliffs looking for somewhere to land. But the cliffs remained unbroken and perversely sheer. They were not especially high—no more than forty or fifty feet in most places—and I dare say that the three of us could have scaled them if we had set our minds to it; but there was no way up for huskies and sledge. By seven o'clock the dogs were tiring —which was not to be wondered at, since they had covered a full fifty miles since breakfast. We therefore decided to postpone trying to get ashore until the morrow, and to pitch camp for the night on the sea-ice. This was no hardship—indeed, many people prefer camping on sea-ice to camping on land, because over the sea there tends to be less drifting of snow. We therefore kept our eyes open for a good site, and before long I was hauling the dogs to a halt in the center of a large and pleasantly sheltered bay.

We were quite expert by this time in setting up Meade tent and snow wall; and Ross and Somerville had cottoned on to several of the old trappers' dodges—such as building the wall a few inches lower than the roof of the tent, so that a thin layer of snow collected on the canvas, insulating and preventing flapping. Within a hour of halting, tent and snow wall were up, and we were sitting in the near-heatless but cheerful sunlight watching our supper of Arctic hare aboil over the Primus.

It was a beautiful evening: very still and very quiet, with the westering sun low-slung and casting long purple shadows across the bay. There was no sign of life; no movement, except on a far-off headland where a sunset wind streamed snow-plumes off the top of the cliffs.

After supper we settled down to look at our maps of Prince Patrick Island. We had, of course, studied them often enough before: but now that we were camped in the island's shadow they took on a new significance. They told us aggravatingly little. For the fact was this: Prince Patrick Island had never been explored—indeed. it seemed probably that no one had ever set foot on it. It lay far to the west of the Arctic air route and far to the north of the D.E.W. Line radar posts; and little was known about it except its rough outline—mapped first by the Stefansson Expedition of 1908-12, and later by the Arctic Air Survey of 1949-50. And even this outline was partly conjecture: for in each case survey work in the north had been hampered by mist. In fact all that was known of the island's structure and conformation is shown on the sketch map.

It was while we were studying the map and Stefansson's report on his expedition (a copy of which Somerville had procured on loan from the Royal Geographical Society Library) that I first became conscious of the feeling which was to haunt us so persistently in the days to come: the feeling of being watched. Surprised, I straightened up and looked at the island. Nothing moved. But the shadows were longer now, darker, and were reaching out like black fingers towards the tent. Unaccountably I shivered. I said nothing to the others; for there seemed no point in alarming them needlessly. But it wasn't long before I noticed Somerville, usually the most placid of men, start, and look anxiously over his shoulder. The Factor's warnings about Prince Patrick Island came back to me then: with renewed significance.

By ten o'clock the sun had dropped under the rim of the cliffs; the bay was in shadow now, and in the north the sky was already streaked with a faint luminosity—an indication of the *aurora borealis* to come. We sat round the fire, talking of this and that, curiously loth to turn in.

It was Ross who, in his usual forthright manner, voiced the fear that we were all of us privately worried by. Suddenly, in the middle of a conversation, he jumped to his feet. His voice was sharp.

"We're being watched!"

I took out my pipe. "Watched? Who could be watching us?"

"Must be the Factor's men with yellow hair." He was half-joking, half-serious.

"Winter Harbour," I said slowly, "is the last of the settlements. Nobody lives north of Winter Harbour; not even nomadic Eskimo: let alone men with yellow hair."

"Then why are we acting like three scairt old women?"

I warmed my hands round the bowl of my pipe. "All this"—I gestured at the vast and empty snowscape surrounding us—"all this has a funny effect on people. It's easy to start imagining things."

The others, I could see, were unconvinced.

"Listen," I said, "and I'll tell you about an old trapper I knew who got snowed up on the Mackenzie." I leaned forward and pushed another block of fuel into the Primus. "A man of fifty to fifty-five, he'd have been: a pleasant, level-headed sort of chap. Well, there he was, caught one autumn by an unlucky run of blizzards over three hundred miles from the nearest village. But he wasn't specially worried; he'd plenty of food, you see, and plenty of furs to keep warm in; so he built himself an igloo, and settled down to see out the winter. To start with everything was fine. But after five or six weeks he began to hear things: things a man shouldn't be hearing: the voice of a little girl, whispering. He'd sit in his igloo hour after hour, he told me afterwards, listening, wondering, growing more and more frightened, until he couldn't bear it any longer and he'd go rushing into the open, convinced there was someone outside the igloo. To start with there was never anyone there. But one day"—I took a couple of longish draws at my pipe—"one day he saw her. A naked little Eskimo girl, dancing round and round the igloo.

"Well, to cut a long story short, the old trapper just about went off his head. For the whispering went on, day and night, week after week; and whenever he looked outside there was the little Eskimo dream girl, dancing away in the snow, smiling at him, trying to tempt him away from the igloo. By mid-February he'd had all he could take. He packed up and ran." I paused. "When he sledged into Port Brabant six weeks later, his hair was white as a polar bear's; he'd lost six toes and a hand with frostbite; and he swore that all the way down from the Mackenzie a naked little Eskimo girl had been dancing round and round his sledge."

There was an astonished silence; then Somerville helped himself to snuff.

"That's all very well," he said. "But your trapper friend was alone. There are three of us."

I nodded. "All the same, it proves what imagination can do."

We stared at the cliffs of Prince Patrick Island, somber and grey-black in the twilight. Then Ross smacked a fist into the palm of his hand.

"I don't believe it!" He began to pace up and down. "Why should we all imagine the same thing? Some coincidence! I say we *are* being watched."

This had to be scotched. For I knew that in the Arctic (as on a high mountain) little differences and little fears had a habit of boiling up to explosive climaxes.

"Tell you what," I said quickly. "I don't believe for a moment there's anyone watching us. But we'll take no chances. From now on we'll keep together: we'll keep the Sten guns loaded; and we'll keep a look-out, turn and turn about."

The others brightened visibly at this; and we straightway divided the night into three watches of three hours each. Somerville and I then turned in, leaving the captain and his Sten gun to protect us from "ghoulies and ghosties and things that go bump in the night." And I must admit that the scrunch of his footsteps as they circled the Meade tent was a very comforting sound to drop off to sleep to.

I relieved Ross at 1 A.M. The night was bitterly cold, but visibility was good—in an Arctic summer the nights are never completely dark, and even at 1 A.M. there's a paleness around the horizon; also, any brightness there happens to be from moon, aurora or stars is reflected and magnified by the great expanse of snow.

"All quiet?" I asked him.

He nodded and passed over the Sten gun—which I noticed with some surprise was cocked. We exchanged a few words about the need to keep condensation off the gun barrel, then he crawled into the tent. For some minutes I heard him moving about, taking off his boots, punching up his sleeping bag. Then there was silence: absolute silence.

I slung the Sten gun over my shoulder and began to

pace up and down. Prince Patrick Island lay sleeping under the stars. The moon shadows were a pale anaemic grey. The cliffs surrounding our camp were ebony black. And it wasn't long before I discovered why Ross had cocked the Sten gun. The feeling of being watched was quite overpowering. I peered at the outline of Prince Patrick Island, until my eyes watered with the strain of probing the shadows; but I could see no sign of life, no movement. In all the starlit icebound world the only moving thing was my shadow, circling the Meade tent like some pale disembodied wraith. Now I am not, I think, of a specially nervous temperament; but I must admit that I was thoroughly relieved when at 3 A.M. the sun came welling over the horizon, flooding the bay with shafts of light. For once I could see more clearly, I felt braver by far—we are all, I think, children at heart: afraid of the unknown monster that lies await in the dark.

Yet glad as I was to see the sun up, its advent didn't entirely dispel my fears. For the feeling of being pried on remained. It was a feeling I still had when at 4 A.M., I handed over to Somerville; and I still had it three hours later when I woke and set about helping the others cook breakfast and feed the dogs.

We struck camp early that morning, in the hope that the business of sledging would chase our apprehension away. And to a certain extent it did. By eight-thirty we were again heading south, following the line of the cliffs (which remained unclimbable and remarkably constant in height); and for some time we were too busy to worry about whether or not we were being watched. For although sledging *looks* easy, it is in fact extremely arduous —especially north of 75, where the intense cold puts a premium on physical effort. All that morning we took turn and turn about at breaking the trail, steering the sledge, and keeping an eye on the shore. Breaking trail was a sinecure; one simply skied ahead of the sledge and parallel to the line of the cliffs: not too close—for the inshore ice could be treacherous; and not too far away—for we wanted no cleft or inlet, however small, to escape our scrutiny. Steering was the most popular job, for driving huskies is always exhilarating; but it was also the coldest;

after a very few minutes one's glove tended to freeze to the steering bar, and one was for ever changing hands and trying to restore one's circulation. The third job—keeping an eye on the shore—was the most exhausting. For although it seemed pretty certain that with cliffs dropping sheer to the sea-ice we'd find no graveyard of the whales in this part of the island, we were taking no chances; and every little bay and inlet was scrupulously skied into. And there was one other job we had: one that was self-appointed, one that we never talked about. We all of us, all the time, kept a wary eye on the top of the cliffs.

For the feeling of being watched—and watched by something malignant—never left us. I don't mean that we were conscious of it all the time; but always at the back of our minds the feeling was there, ready at the least provocation to make itself felt. A cloud shadow passing over the sledge, and we'd look anxiously up: an avalanche rumbling inland, and we'd start and peer suspiciously at the cliffs. Yet neither that day nor for several days to come did we see any tangible indication that the island might be inhabited.

Then, as we were approaching the island's south-east tip, there came an unexpected piece of excitement.

We had halted as usual at midday, and, since the wind was keen, Somerville and I decided to throw up a windbreak, while Ross heated the cocoa. It was while we were stacking snow-blocks into a wall that I first noticed the isolated protuberance only two or three hundred yards from where we had camped. It was the one hummock in a vast expanse of ice which stretched, smooth as a skating rink, as far as the eye could see. My first thought was that it must be caused by snow drifting against an upthrust rock. Then, struck by a sudden fear, I went across to the sledge and unearthed the binoculars. After a long look at the hummock, I handed the glasses to Somerville.

"What do you make of that?"

In the magnified circle the protuberance stood out in detail: a bank of snow lodged against something solid, rectangular and black: something which looked more like metal than rock.

Somerville moistened his lips. "Could be the helicopter."

I nodded. I glanced at Ross, busy heating the cocoa.

"Come on," I said. "You and I'll have a look."

As we hurried across to the mound, all sorts of grue-some visions came welling up in my mind: visions of shat-tered wreckage, twisted metal, a broken body. But as we drew closer, I realized in a flood of relief that it wasn't the whole helicopter which lay in the snow; it was only part of it: one of its jettisoned long-range fuel tanks. We stared in silence at the sixty-gallon stainless-steel container, re-minder of a world that seemed very far away.

"It was because of the long-range tanks," I said slowly, "that we knew young Ross's flight was premeditated. They weren't usually carried."

We were levering the container out of the snow, when I noticed Ross running anxiously towards us.

"It's all right," I sang out. "It's only a fuel tank."

His face crumpled up in relief and he slowed down to a walk. "Thank God for that. I thought maybe he'd crashed."

We hauled the tank upright; it was surprisingly heavy. We hammered off the refuelling cap—it was too frozen up to unscrew; and out, in a pale gold flood, gushed the pet-rol. The tank was nearly half full.

Now here was a mystery! Young Ross, even with extra tanks, would have had little enough fuel to get to Prince Patrick Island and back. Why on earth should he jettison a tank which was only half empty? Our eyes were drawn, unwillingly, to the cliffs of Prince Patrick Island. But the cliffs told us nothing. Enigmatic as ever, whatever secrets they had they didn't disclose.

We left the fuel tank where we had found it—there was nothing else we could do with it. We heated and drank our cocoa. Then we whipped up the dogs and sledged on. And soon the tiny rectangle of black was swallowed up in the whiteness of ice and snow.

Well, the finding of the tank—and the fact that it was still half full—certainly gave us food for thought. It was our first bit of concrete evidence, too, that the expedition was something more than a wild-goose chase. And yet, it seemed to me, its discovery wasn't an event of very great significance; for it told us nothing new; it merely confirmed what we already suspected. Ross, on the other hand, obviously thought differently. The finding of the tank acted as a whetstone to the edge of his hope; and it was clear that from now on he was more than ever convinced—against all the evidence and all the odds—that he was going to find his son.

In the next couple of days there were no further excitements; but we made excellent progress. We rounded Prince Patrick Island's south-east tip; and by Tuesday, 25 August, were approaching Mould Bay—a great inlet cut deep into the southern coast. In just one week we had covered 178 miles, had sledged a quarter of the way round the island, and had come to one of the likeliest places for finding the graveyard—a fjord-like waterway facing south, fed by a glacial stream, and with its entrance close to the edge of the summer pack ice.

We camped that evening in the mouth of the inlet. And it wasn't long before the old familiar feeling of being spied on came creeping over us: unaccountable, inexplicable, insidious as marsh gas filtering out through the pores of a swamp. We were, by this time, so accustomed to the feeling that we hardly discussed it. (We had each evolved our own theory to account for it. I put it down to imagination; Ross was convinced there really was someone spying on us; and the professor had some complicated idea of his own which he didn't want to discuss without evidence.) We did, however, comment on the fact that the sensation was more overpowering, that evening, than usual—and this I put down to the claustrophobic effect of the cliffs lining the fjord, which were somber and forbidding in the extreme.

We were all three unusually restless that night and slept badly—in spite of the fact that we were still keeping watch turn and turn about. And as soon as I woke in the morning I sensed that something was wrong. One look outside, and I reached for the barometer. It had fallen seven points in as many hours.

As we set about striking camp, everything was very still and very quiet. The air was unnaturally clear; the cliffs looked close-to and larger than life; and the sun was shining with a sort of desperate intensity (as though it knew it wouldn't be shining for long). There was every indication, in fact, that we were in for a summer blizzard.

"Mush!" I cracked the sealskin dog-whip.

And we shot into the fjord at a spanking gallop.

Mould Bay, according to our maps, went tapering inland for close on thirty miles. It was lined by sheer hundred-foot cliffs of Proterozoic rock, black as shale, and—to judge from the debris along their base—no more stable. To start with the cliffs were several miles apart; but as we progressed inland, they drew closer together; until by midday we were sledging down a mere riband of ice—in perpetual shadow—with the cliffs so close to each other that they seemed almost to meet overhead. It was an eerie place: made eerier still by the oppressive silence, and by the feeling of being spied on. As I looked up at the rampartlike defenses of Prince Patrick Island (which had remained unclimbable ever since we had set eyes on them) I couldn't help shivering. No wonder, I thought, the Eskimoes were scared stiff of the island: no wonder they held it taboo.

Our progress down the fjord was slow. We wanted to avoid overhangs and unstable screes; but we also wanted to make our survey a hundred per cent conclusive. And so all that morning, and all afternoon too, we groped our snail-like way along the foot of the cliffs, peering into clefts and inlets, crevices and caves. We examined every foot of both sides of the fjord. But of whales, either dead or alive, we found no trace.

We were feeling weary and somewhat depressed when, towards evening, the cliffs fell abruptly away; and rounding a bend we saw ahead of us a scene of the utmost grandeur.

Up from the foot of Mould Bay there wound a broad glacial valley, its séracs and ice pinnacles aglint in the evening sun. Inland, the hills on either side of the valley rose steeply; but lower down, where the glacial moraine debouched into the fjord, an apron of level ground lay, like a semi-circular terrace, between sea-ice and hills. And the approaches to the terrace were slopes of snow: gentle, obviously climbable. Here, at last, was a way ashore. We whipped up the dogs.

Ross, eager to be first to set foot on the island, skied on

ahead. He scrambled up to the terrace; he tossed a handful of snow into the air.

"Prince Patrick Island!" His shout echoed back from the hills. "Prince Patrick Island! At last!"

I looked at him anxiously, with a vague expectation that some terrible fate would dart at him from out of the snow. But nothing happened, save that an avalanche rumbled faintly among the far-off hills of the hinterland.

Soon we were all ashore, searching for a camp site. There wasn't a great deal of choice over this, for the terrace of level ground was less than a hundred yards wide. But we eventually found a pleasant enough spot, nicely sheltered behind some lumps of moraine. Here we set up the Meade tent.

Rather to my surprise we didn't experience, that evening, our usual sensation of being pried on. And this, I told myself, was probably because we had something else to think about: the weather.

For all day the glass had been falling fast.

There were other signs too, that evening, that the fine spell was breaking. The wind, aback from north to east; the dampness in the air; and, high in the sky, the small white tendrils of cirrus, harbingers of the approaching front. I decided we'd best build an igloo; for I knew that in a full-scale blizzard the Meade tent would be no more use than the little pig's house of straw.

Now there is quite an art in building an igloo. If it is done with big ill-fitting snow-blocks, the roof—as I'd discovered by bitter experience—invariably caves in. I therefore made certain that evening that Ross and Somerville cut and dovetailed in only the smallest and most carefully graded of blocks. The result was that progress was painfully slow, and it was midnight before the domelike sections of the roof were ready to meet overhead. But at least, as we dovetailed in the last of the snow-wedges, we had the satisfaction of knowing we'd done a workmanlike job.

And it was as well we had. For early that morning the wind began to slam up and down the fjord, ripping great snow-plumes off the face of the cliffs; banks of cumulus, marching up from the south, were soon flooding like spilt ink over the sun; and a little before midday the first of the snow-flakes came swirling out of a lead-grey sky.

64

The dogs knew what was coming; they curled up in the lee of the igloo, only the tips of their noses above the snow. We collapsed the Meade tent. Stores, guns, Primus and fuel we carried into the igloo. And we were none too soon. For by mid-afternoon a full-scale blizzard was raging over the island.

We lay in our sleeping bags listening to the wind: a continual wavering moan, rising every now and then to a high-pitched shriek. Outside, banners of whipped-up snow streamed near-horizontal over the ice. But inside, we were warm and sheltered and content. Indeed, paradoxically enough, we were happier than we had been for days. For the blizzard had swept away all trace of our apprehension and fears, and we no longer felt we were being watched over, pried on by a mysterious "something" we didn't understand. The dangers we now had to face were concrete physical dangers: wind and snow and cold. And of this we were glad.

All that day the blizzard continued. And the next day. And the next.

Those who have never been in an Arctic snow-storm can have little idea of its sustained ferocity. Day after day wind comes clawing out of the darkness, never slackening, never letting up. Day after day snow comes plastering down, ton after ton to the square yard, as malevolent and unremitting as the wind. We stayed inside. To have ventured out would have been suicide. When we felt we needed a breath of air, we crawled to the mouth of the igloo, and lay gazing at a scene which had lost its usual component parts of land and sea and sky, and had shrunk to a single kaleidoscopic mêlée, in which snow and ice and clouds were merged into one frenetic whirlwind blown streaming off the roof of the world.

It was a full seventy-two hours before the blizzard showed signs of lifting. Then, during its fourth night, the barometer shot suddenly up; and by dawn on September 1 the snow had slackened, the wind had dropped, and a watery sun began to gleam intermittently through breaks in the cloud. We crawled out of the igloo.

Once in the open we rubbed our eyes in astonishment. For the world, during our hibernation, had been re-

65

molded. The fjord, which we remembered as a deep ravine, was now choked bank-high with driven snow. The surrounding hills, once precipitous, were now smoothly rounded, their contours softened by the all-enveloping mantle of white. It was like walking into a dream world, full of half-remembered objects which were somehow not quite right. We paced up and down, taking in our new surroundings, and glad of the chance to stretch our legs. After a while we brought out the Primus and brewed up some tea; then we set to to dig out Meade tent and sledge.

We were shoveling away at the snow, and had excavated to a depth of several feet without finding anything, when Ross gave a sudden gasp.

"Look!"

His arm was flung out, pointing to the hills above the igloo.

Somerville and I spun round. We could see nothing. And yet the captain was adamant; he was convinced he'd seen men: two of them, high on a spur of the hills; and the moment, he said, he'd straightened up to point at them, they had dodged back beneath the skyline.

"Men!" I was incredulous. "But there *can't* be anyone else on the island!"

"How about the men with yellow hair?"

Silence. And as we stared at the encircling hills, all our old unease came surging back, like flood water arise behind the walls of a dam. And yet I couldn't believe he had *really* seen anyone.

"You must have imagined it."

He shook his head. "No. I didn't imagine it." His voice was quiet, matter-of-fact; and somehow it carried more conviction than the most vehement of tirades.

Somerville helped himself to snuff. "Men or no men"— he eyed the snow-covered hills—"it mightn't be a bad idea to shift camp."

I could see what he was thinking. For four days the snow had fallen without respite. The gullies were choked with it now: the cwms were overflowing: and down from the cliffs surrounding our camp the cornices hung in heavy festoons, like pastry draped round the edge of a pie-dish. The sun was shining too; it was perfect avalanche weather.

I didn't like the idea of being driven out of our camp by

66

the fear of being spied on—apart from anything else it created a precedent, and a fine expedition we'd make if we packed up and ran at every suspect shadow. But to move camp through fear of an avalanche, on the other hand . . . that was no more than common prudence.

"O.K.," I said slowly, "we'll look for another site. Right away."

The going, I knew, after so much snow, would be heavy. We therefore agreed to make the move in two stages. First, we'd load the sledge with a few necessities (such as Meade tent and Primus) and make a reconnaissance; then, when we'd found a site, we'd come back for the main bulk of provisions and stores.

It was a lovely afternoon as we pulled away from the igloo. The clouds had lifted, the sun was shining and the snow turned out to be crisp and reasonably firm. We sledged away from the hills, glad to be doing something positive after our days of inactivity. At the first bend in the valley we paused and looked back at the igloo.

"I suppose it's all right to leave it?" Somerville sounded doubtful.

The same thought had occurred to me. But as I looked up-valley I saw a small saddle jutting bastionlike into the glacier. I pointed it out to the others. "Looks like a good site. We'll be there and back in twenty minutes."

We pushed on, the dogs sinking belly-deep in the freshly fallen snow, and after a stiff haul gained the saddle. From here we had a magnificent view, both of the glacier, and, over the top of the moraine, down through the fjord and out to sea. We were sledging about, looking for a good spot to set up the Meade tent, when a sudden roar jerked us to a halt. The roar deepened; it went on and on, an angry vibrating rumble, gathering momentum.

"An avalanche!" Ross's voice was a whisper.

"At the foot of the valley, too." Somerville moistened his lips.

"Come on!" I shouted. "Quick!"

Spurred on by the same fear, we whipped up the dogs and went racing back down-valley. Rounding the bend we pulled up short.

"My God!" whispered Ross.

It was a peaceful scene we looked down on. There

wasn't a sign of the catacylsmic forces of destruction which a few minutes before had engulfed the foot of the valley. Only the scars remained: the three weal-like avalanche trails which swept from hilltop to fjord, obliterating whatever lay in their path. And one of the things in their path had been our igloo. Over sixty per cent of our stores. And all our food. We stood a long time in silence: the implications sinking slowly in.

"Come on," I said at last. "Let's see if there's anything left."

Keeping a wary eye on the hills, we skied down to what had once been a camp. But nothing was there. Absolutely nothing. Igloo and stores alike had been swept headlong into the fjord. We picked our way down to the shore, hoping that something might have lodged on the sea-ice. But the sea-ice lay shattered into myriad fragments, broken by the weight of the avalanche snow. All we found was the splintered frame of a packing case, the stem of a snowshoe, and a single tin of cocoa, badly crushed.

As we plodded back to where we had left the dogs, I studied the tracks of the avalanches. They started from three quite separate points, and yet they converged with the igloo. They were no accident. That much was obvious.

I turned to Ross. "You were right," I said "And I was wrong. We *were* being watched."

We sledged the rest of the way back to the saddle in silence. We set up the Meade tent—in a spot commanding a good view and well out of range of any possible avalanche. Then, while Somerville mounted guard, Ross and I made an inventory of what was left of our stores. The inventory was soon made. All that was left was the tent, the Primus and fuel, our snowshoes and skis, two spades and a length of rope, our navigational equipment, nine blankets and three sleeping bags, a few odd clothes, two dozen sticks of dynamite, and the Sten guns and rifles; also a few oddments of food which we salvaged from various pockets and the bottom of the sledge. This food we piled together carefully on top of one of the sleeping bags. And a pathetically meagre pile it made: about three pounds of dog meat, five bars of chocolate, one tin of condensed milk, one "escaper's pack" of concentrated vitamin tablets, and two and a half tins of cocoa. Ross and I looked at each other.

He moistened his lips. "That won't get us back to Winter Harbour."

"No," I said slowly, "it certainly won't."

7

A Whisper of Aspen Leaves

WE were in trouble, serious trouble; and I couldn't see any way out of it. Indeed, the more I thought things over the more desperate our situation appeared.

We sat round the Primus hour after hour, discussing what to do next; and in the end we boiled the alternatives down to three. (I) We could try and get back to Winter Harbour. (II) We could go on trying to find the graveyard. (III) We could stay where we were and hope to meet up with the caribou.

(I) was the obvious choice; and the one we'd have taken, I think, if it hadn't been for the freshly fallen snow which made sledging doubly exhausting and more than doubly slow. We worked it out carefully, so many miles and so much food per day; and the fact was this: even if we had perfect weather, and even if we killed off and ate the dogs *en route* we couldn't get back. Somewhere, about a hundred and fifty miles short of Winter Harbour we'd kill our last dog, drink our last cup of cocoa, and that would be that.

(II) found no supporters. We didn't even know for sure that the graveyard existed; and if it did exist, we didn't know where. And once again, even if we killed off and ate the dogs, we'd run out of food long before we'd circumnavigated the island.

That left us with (III).

"Suppose the Factor was wrong"—this was Somerville—"Suppose the caribou never turn up?"

"He seemed quite definite about them." I thought back to my talk—it seemed very long ago—in the Company store. "He told me he'd seen 'em himself. That they always hit the island the same time of year—round about now. And that they always headed up through Mould Bay. If we can believe him, they ought to pass within a few hundred yards of where we're camped."

Silence, while we weighed the odds. Then Ross said slowly, "I say we ought to believe the Factor. He was right about the men with yellow hair. Odds are he'll be right about the caribou."

Somerville nodded. "With one proviso, I'm with you. We ought to check that the caribou haven't already passed."

"Check? How can we?"

"Dig down to the reindeer moss. See if it's eaten."

Of course. I ought to have thought of it myself. If the herd had already passed, the moss would be cropped short as a lawn.

Leaving Ross, armed with a Sten gun, to mount guard over the tent, the professor and I skied down to the foot of the valley. We chose a strip of low-lying ground; we stacked our rifles, unslung our spades, and started to dig. We dug fast—knowing that our lives very likely depended on what we found under the snow. And four feet down we came to the moss, the many-branched *cladonia rangiferina,* spread like a lichen carpet over the barrens. And its shoots were mercifully long and tender. The caribou were still to come. Just to be a hundred per cent certain of this, we skied a little way farther up-valley and tried again; and again the moss was uneaten.

We climbed back, almost cheerfully, to the Meade tent; and decided there and then to pin our faith in the Factor being right, to stay in our camp overlooking the valley and wait for the caribou.

"Only God Grant," I said, as we turned in for the night, "that we don't have to wait for long."

Our first step next morning was to start building our-

71

selves an igloo. Only a few hundred yards along the saddle we discovered an idyllic site: a shallow cwm, sheltered on three sides and with a magnificent view over the valley on the fourth. In the center of this cwm we built our snow-house. We took a long time building it. We had, after all, nothing else to do. Our second step was to work out a minimum daily ration. Assuming that we killed one husky every three days, I reckoned we could count on one hot meal of dog meat and lichen, a half mug of unsweetened cocoa and two small squares of chocolate every twenty-four hours. Based on this consumption (which I estimated was the minimum, in the intense cold, to keep us alive) our supplies would last just under three weeks. Our third step was to agree on a rota of watches—both as a precaution against unwelcome visitors and as a look-out for the caribou. We also agreed that each evening one of us would climb the hills behind the camp and survey the shore on either side of Mould Bay, in case the herd picked a different place to land.

Having decided all this there was nothing we could do but wait.

To start with, time passed almost pleasantly. We did a great deal of talking. (There was little else we could do, since anything that involved physical effort sapped our strength and sharpened our appetite.) And one of the first things we talked about was the mystery of our unseen watchers—who, by the way, we suspected were still keeping an eye on us.

Both Ross and I advanced theories of a sort to try and account for them. But Somerville, it turned out, had all the answers already weighed up. He had, he told us quietly, been thinking the problem over ever since the first night we had met aboard the *Dunvegan*.

The captain and I gasped at this. "But you didn't know they existed then!" I exclaimed.

He smiled, and went on to explain it all so simply, step by logical step, that I could only wonder I hadn't figured it out for myself—there, I suppose, lies the difference between a clever man and a foolish one; both see the same facts, but only the former sees how to use them!

"Remember the old parchment, dated 1672?" Somerville fished out a sheaf of typewritten notes from among his charts. "Listen: *'With the NativeS waS a younge girl who had yellow hair, and whom I took at firSt for a white woman.'* He only 'took her for a white woman,' you notice, at first; she wasn't one really; and if that's so, there's only one thing she could have been: a blonde Eskimo." He paused. "Now I looked up Blond Eskimo in the *Encyclopaedia Britannica,* and I found this." He thumbed through his notes. "Here we are." He quoted: 'The so-called Blond Eskimo were first reported by the Stefansson Expedition of 1908-12. They appear to consist of nomadic tribes inhabiting Coronation Gulf and the Southwest Parry Islands. It is a matter of dispute whether they are of pure North American origin, tainted by intermarriage with whites, or whether they are descendants of the Norse colonists who occupied Greenland in the Middle Ages.' " Another pause, while this sank in; then he went on. "Well, the next step was obvious. I looked up Stefansson's account of his expedition"—so that, I thought, was why he had spent so long in the Pangnirtung library—"and I found the truth of the matter was this. Stefansson only saw the Blond Eskimoes twice. On the first occasion he found a whole family—mother, father and two young boys—frozen to death in an igloo. On the second occasion he spotted a party of fifteen or twenty, sledging over the sea-ice; but they made off before he could get near enough to question them. Both times he was off the north coast of Prince Patrick Island.

"So the facts look like this. In 1672 a Company Factor sees an Eskimo girl with yellow hair who he is told, comes from Prince Patrick Island, and whom the other Eskimoes 'durst not take home.' In 1910 Stefansson spots two lots of yellow-haired Eskimoes close to Prince Patrick Island. Now, in 1959, we're warned that if we go to Prince Patrick Island we're to 'look out for men with yellow hair'; as soon as we near the island we feel we're being watched, and as soon as we set foot on it, somebody tries to finish us off with an avalanche. Seems to me it all adds up to one thing: a tribe of Blond Eskimoes live on Prince Patrick Island and want to keep the place to themselves."

It was like one of those annoying little puzzles with loops and bent nails; all so obvious when someone points out how and why.

"And if that's the case," I said, as the thought suddenly occurred to me, "I'll hazard a pretty good guess where the

Blond Eskimoes live: next to the graveyard. Where else, this far north, could they get food?"

It was a strange set-up all right. We discussed it all that night, and on and off for days to come. And in the end we came to two conclusions. First, the most likely place for the graveyard now seemed to be Black Bay, on the north coast of the island, where mist had hampered survey work and where Stefansson had spotted the two lots of yellow-haired Eskimoes. Second, it was quite on the cards that the caribou were heading towards the graveyard. For unless there was some special attraction in the north of the island, why should they be heading that way, when their usual migratory course in the autumn was south by east? So, if we followed the caribou, they might well lead us to the graveyard. It all added up to the fact that once the herd turned up, it looked like being roses, roses all the way.

But alas for our sanguine hopes! The herd didn't turn up.

The days passed. They lengthened to weeks. And of the longed-for caribou there was never a sign.

We lay in our igloo. Hour after hour. Day after day. Waiting. Growing gradually weaker, gradually more depressed as our stocks of food and our expectation of life drained inexorably away. By mid-September we had killed and eaten half the dogs, and were down to our last tin of cocoa and our last bar of chocolate.

Now it isn't easy to be brave when one is perpetually cold and perpetually hungry, and starting to go snow-blind into the bargain. But Ross and Somerville were magnificent. It would have been quite excusable if they had turned against me. I was, after all, the expedition leader; and I had led them step by step to disaster. Yet they didn't reproach me; there were no recriminations, no post-mortems on what we ought to have done; they simply accepted what was happening as inevitable, as the price which those who venture into the unknown must always be prepared to pay.

Soon we were too weak to climb the hills overlooking the valley. Too weak, too, to mount a guard. We simply lay in our sleeping bags, hour after hour, waiting. Our only move was when one of us, every now and then, would crawl to the mouth of the igloo and stare hopefully down-valley. But the valley always looked the same: cold as the stars, silent as sleep, motionless as death.

I think that Somerville's Diary paints a more vivid picture of those terrible days in the igloo than could any words of mine.

Friday, Sept. 18th. Fine but v. cold. Killed another husky; only 5 left now. Ross troubled by snow-blindness, due to lack of vitamin C. Persuaded him to have extra mugful of boiled lichen.

Saturday, Sept. 19th. All of us much weaker this morning. Ross partially snow-blind, and dogs v. restless —I suppose with hunger. Rogers says if the caribou don't come within 48 hrs., it looks like the end.

It's funny, I don't remember saying that. But I do remember thinking, as I curled up for the night, how much kinder it would be if none of us woke the next morning.

I woke suddenly. Moonlight was flooding in through the walls of the igloo, and the dogs were baying their heads off.

I lay on my back, trying to summon up sufficient energy to go and see what was wrong. After a while I gave up. It was so much simpler to lie in the comparative warmth of my sleeping bag, and try to analyze the different sounds. The howl of the dogs was loud and unmistakable; so was their pant and scrabble as they jerked at their leads. I could recognize, too, the hum of the wind as it came streaming over the rim of the cwm. But there was another sound as well, a sound which puzzled me, a sound like the whisper of aspen leaves astir in a summer breeze. I had heard it somewhere before: long, long ago: but I couldn't remember where. It seemed hardly worth the effort to conjure the memory up, and I began to slide back into the twilit world of fantasy and dream, where hunger, exhaustion and physical weakness were unimportant, and problems (like inexplicable noises) needed no logical explanation. Then I remembered. Remembered where, long ago, the aspen leaves had whispered. I started to tremble then. It couldn't, I thought, be true. It was a cruel delusion: like the oasis seen in a sea of sand by a man who is dying of thirst. I listened, expecting the whisper to die away. But it didn't. It went on and on, never rising, never falling, filling the night.

I rolled out of the sleeping bag. I scrambled out of the igloo.

The dogs were mad with excitement. Their eyes flamed like rubies; their mouths were aslobber, and they were choking themselves against the pull of their leads. I looked out across the snow; and there, coming over the edge of the cwm, silhouetted in the gold of the moonlight, was the most wonderful sight I have ever seen. The ghosts on the skyline. The hundred-thousand herd of Alaskan caribou streaming close-packed up the valley. They moved silently, like well-oiled two-dimensional silhouettes; their slotted hooves made no sound on the snow; but their antlers, rubbing together, whispered like aspen leaves astir in a summer breeze.

I am not what you would call a religious man—few whalers are—but there and then I dropped to my knees in the snow and gave thanks to God. Then I slipped the dogs and scrambled back to the igloo. I grabbed hold of Somerville, whom the hullabaloo had woken.

"Come on!" I shouted. "Caribou!"

He didn't believe me at first. He thought I was delirious. And no wonder, for I was near-hysterical with excitement and relief. But I half dragged him out of the igloo; and then he saw for himself the grey unending column spilling like a river in flood into the valley. We both felt damnably weak—what with excitement and lack of food—but we grabbed our guns, and leaving Ross asleep in a semi-coma, struggled up the cwm. The snow-slope was very gentle; but it was almost more than we could manage.

"Won't they see us," Somerville panted, "and scatter?"

I shook my head. Nothing, I knew, would disrupt the migrating caribou. If a bomb burst in the middle of them, they would simply close up their ranks and plod on. Down in the valley we saw our dogs, worrying at the fringe of the column, trying to prize a fawn away from its parents. Even as we watched, one of the youngsters was singled out, was dragged down, the dogs at its throat. We struggled to within twenty yards of the column. A few of the caribou raised their heads to look at us: their liquid eyes gazed at us blankly: unafraid.

76

"Pick the young ones," I panted. "Take your time, and aim a little behind the shoulder."

We raised our guns. The rifle cracked; the Sten gun clattered; the echoes ricocheted around the cwm, and the snow was stained blood-red. But the caribou never faltered; they closed their ranks and plodded unconcernedly on. It was the slaughter of the innocent. In ten minutes we shot twenty-three. We could, if we had wanted to, have gone on; but there was no need. There on the blood-stained snow lay meat enough for several months; and if, later, we needed more, the caribou would still be there for the killing—for I knew it would take several days for the herd to pass.

As we dragged the smallest of our kill back to the igloo, Ross, woken by the sound of gun-fire, came staggering out to meet us.

The joy of that morning is past describing. We were men who had walked in the valley of the shadow of death, and who had come, contrary to all expectations, out of the valley and back to their own familiar world. Everything we did, we did with a thankful incredulity. Everything we said, we said with a touch of awe. All morning we ate and talked and ate and laughed, and ate and let the snow run through our fingers. We were so very thankful to be alive. Later there might be doubts and qualifications—the fact that Ross was partially snow-blind, the fact that the last of our dogs were rampaging among the caribou—but for the moment we put these things from our minds. The sun shone; we were able to feel its warmth; and that for the moment was all that mattered.

All day we stayed close to our igloo, happy to rest in the sun and know that food—as much as we wanted—was ours for the taking. And that night, for the first time in weeks, we slept deeply, lulled to a sense of well-being by the rustle of antlers, as the caribou, hour after hour, streamed close-packed into the valley.

Next morning came the inevitable reaction. We had over-eaten, and now we had to pay for it; Ross's eyes were throbbing painfully, and the dogs were still missing. We came down to earth with a bump. But we now had the spirit and the resources to tackle our problems with some vigor; and after a carefully abstemious breakfast I set out

77

to look for the dogs, while the others stayed behind to skin the caribou.

My job proved unexpectedly easy. About a mile down-valley I found the huskies asleep by the caribou trail, gorged to a stupor. I got a rope round Queequeg, the lead-dog, before he was properly awake, and dragged him reluctantly back; the others followed.

I hoped on my return to find a good-sized pile of caribou steaks laid out in the igloo; instead I found Ross and Somerville huddled together in anxious conversation. I could tell that something was wrong.

The second he saw me Somerville jumped up.

"Look at this!"

I followed him up the cwm to where the previous night we had shot the caribou. The carcasses were still there, just as we had left them, dragged into a haphazard pile. But it wasn't the carcases I looked at. It was the arrows that surrounded them: the circle of feathered arrows driven point downward into the snow.

"How the devil did *they* get there?" Somerville was incredulous. "And what do they mean?"

I looked carefully round the cwm, then one at a time I pulled the arrows out. There were twenty-three of them: long vicious-looking weapons, their heads sharp as a razor. And I knew what they meant. A circle is the Eskimo sign for taboo; anyone breaking the circle breaks the taboo; and the penalty for breaking an Eskimo taboo is death.

It took us a couple of hours, hauling and keeping watch in shifts, to drag the carcasses down to the igloo; and a further couple of hours to surround the snow-house with a wall six foot high and thick enough to keep out an arrow. Only then did we get down to discussing just what the warning circle implied.

"As I see it," I said, "the arrows were put there to frighten us off the island. By the men with yellow hair."

"And are we going to be frightened off by a pack of Eskimoes we've never even seen?" Ross, it was clear, was all for pushing on with our search.

"There's more to it," I said slowly, "than that. Much more to it. If all we had to face was a bunch of Eskimoes, I'd not dream of turning back: not for a moment. But we've other things to think of: lack of equipment, lack of

78

balanced food, *and* the fact it's late September now, getting on for winter, in fact."

Out of the corner of my eye I noticed Somerville nodding away in approval. But Ross was indignant.

"Turn back! Just as we're getting somewhere!"

He began to pace up and down. And I realized what he was afraid of. Ever since we had discovered that jettisoned fuel tank, he'd been convinced he was going to find his son; and he was afraid that now, at the eleventh hour, chance of reunion was going to be denied him.

Now my position wasn't easy. It's true I was expedition leader, and I dare say that if I had dug my toes in and insisted we turn back, Ross would have fallen into line. On the other hand, the expedition had been his idea, it had been financed with his money, and it was his son we were looking for.

In the end we hit on a compromise. We would spend a week in the cwm (which I considered the minimum period needed to build up our strength). We would then follow the caribou herd for anything up to a fortnight. If, at the end of that time, they had led us to the graveyard of the whales, we would reconsider our plans; if they hadn't led us there, then we'd have to give up and head back for Winter Harbour.

Having agreed this, we turned in—taking the precaution, of course, of reverting to our usual three-hourly watches. And I for one took my period of sentry duty very seriously indeed. For the men with yellow hair struck me as being dangerous customers.

Two days later the caribou began to thin out. For seventy-two hours they had been streaming into the valley, nose to tail; but now at last the column broke up, until soon only a few stragglers were coming over the edge of the cwm: occasional groups of five or six (mostly does with new-born fawns) hurrying to catch up with the main herd. We were sorry to see them go. They were gentle, harmless creatures, and they had saved our lives. That afternoon the three of us took our guns, and, going to the edge of the cwm, shot another half-dozen of the stragglers. We didn't need them really; but when one has been close to dying of hunger, one is loth to see good food going to waste. In the evening we settled down to skin the carcasses, and by the time we had finished I reckoned we had food for ourselves and the dogs for a good five months. As we were stock-piling the cuts of meat, I noticed a curious stillness had settled over the cwm. I couldn't at first think what had happened. Then I realized that the aspen leaves were no longer whispering. The last of the caribou had gone.

It was about two hours later, while we were having supper, that we first noticed the strange behaviour of the dogs. Their ears were pricked, their eyes were shining, and they were staring up the cwm. I would have thought more caribou were coming if I hadn't known that two herds never follow the same route—for the late-comers would find the lichen already eaten.

"Wolves?" suggested Somerville.

I shook my head.

"We're too far north."

"The men with yellow hair?"

"Could be," I said.

I drew up the fire and checked that the guns were loaded.

"We'd best keep inside the snow wall"—this was Somerville's suggestion.

A few minutes later Queequeg let out a howl: a long-drawn reverberating howl, which echoed and re-echoed round the cwm.

"Listen!" The captain jerked up his head.

Was it echo or answer? Or was it simply our keyed-up imagination? We couldn't be sure; but I for one would have plumped for an answer; a faint far-away answer from the farther side of the valley.

Queequeg, at any rate, seemed satisfied; he lay down in the snow, panting. We looked at each other doubtfully.

"Extra sharp look-out tonight," the captain grunted.

I nodded. "And if we see anything suspicious, shoot first and ask questions after."

It was a funny thing. Blizzard, cold, hunger, even the prospect of death by starvation, we had taken them all, if not in our stride, then at least I liked to think with a certain equanimity; but the thought of the men with yellow hair made us nervous as kittens.

My turn as sentry came around at 11 p.m. It was a beautiful evening, with clouds and stars reeling across a tempestuous sky, and a great copper moon which after a while came swimming over the hills and bathed the valley in a light that was hard and cold and unbelievably bright. The dogs were nervous, and so was I. I kept the fire drawn up. I paced to and fro between the snow wall and igloo, the Sten gun cocked. I felt certain something was going to happen. But the hours passed; the cwm lay silent under the moon, and at 3 a.m. Somerville came out to relieve me.

"Everything quiet," I told him.

Ten minutes later I was rolled up in my sleeping bag, listening to his footsteps circling the igloo. It was a comforting sound: crunch, scrunch, crunch: and soon to its reassuring rhythm I fell asleep. It seemed that my eyes had barely closed (though I found out afterwards that it was really a good two hours later; when the rhythm changed. The crunch, scrunch, crunch gave way to a panicky slap, slap, slap. I sat up, trembling. The flap of the tent was wrenched aside, and Somerville burst into the igloo.

"Quick!" he panted. "Something's coming!"

We grabbed our guns. We tumbled into the open.

The huskies were huddled together, snarling, their eyes aflame, the hackles standing up on their backs like the quills of so many porcupines. And from over the rim of the cwm there came a strange low-pitched hissing, punctuated every now and then by a sharp crack. The noise, subdued but menacing, came swiftly nearer.

It was a noise I had heard before. For a second I was too muddled with sleep and fright to place it. Then I got what it was.

"It's sledges," I said. "Eskimo sledges. Coming fast."

8

"Where the Caribou Can Lead, We Can Follow"

A SECOND later they burst into the cwm: a dozen Eskimo sledges, in loose formation, following the tracks of the caribou. Here I felt certain were the men with the yellow hair, about to launch an attack—and the others admitted afterwards they thought the same. But the Eskimoes didn't attack us. The moment they saw the igloo and snow wall they pulled up short, bunching together on the rim of the cwm like so many frightened sheep.

"Watch out!" I grunted. "May be a trick."

We watched the Eskimoes carefully. They had pulled up about two hundred yards short of us, and it was hard to tell from that distance exactly what was going on. But to all outward appearances they were a bunch of very ordinary and rather frightened Eskimo hunters who had run into something they hadn't bargained for. They huddled together, pointing at our igloo, and jabbering away nineteen to the dozen.

"They're as scared as we are!" Somerville whispered.

Ross lowered his rifle.

"*Those* aren't the men with yellow hair!" He sounded almost disappointed.

We stared at them, uncertain what to do next. It was a queer set-up: the silent cwm bathed in moonlight, and in it the two groups of men who had met in the heart of a supposedly uninhabited island, eight hundred miles inside the Arctic. I handed the Sten gun to Somerville.

"Keep me covered," I said, "in case it's a trick."

He started to remonstrate, but I brushed past him, slipped round the end of the snow wall and started to climb the cwm.

I've never known two hundred yards to seem so far; for I don't mind admitting I was scared stiff. But gradually, as I approached the Eskimoes, my confidence began to come back. For one thing was obvious: they were even more scared of me than I of them! I stopped about twenty yards short of their sledges and waited. There was much whispering together and drawing back; but at last three of them, pushed forward by their companions, came reluctantly towards me.

"Greetings," I said.

"Greetings, O great one."

The tallest and most elderly of the three—whom I took to be some sort of chief—spoke in a dialect I could understand. His voice had a curious deference, and the words "O great one" surprised me. We stared at one another with a mixture of curiosity and suspicion; and it suddenly occurred to me that very likely we were both suspicious about the same thing: the color of each other's hair. I raised my hand to my anorak; slowly I pulled back the hood.

The Eskimoes' eyes widened; then a long-drawn oooooh! of relief came sighing up from the sledges. The chief smiled. He and the man on either side of him also uncovered their heads. And their hair, like mine, was dark.

Our mutual relief was a good basis for establishing friendly relations. We went through the customary semiritual queries about the hunting, the state of each other's health and the local taboos, and soon the four of us were laughing and chattering away without restraint. Once I had gained their confidence I invited them down to the igloo.

Now I didn't want the whole tribe milling round us; for although treachery seemed unlikely it was a possibility that had to be guarded against; so I compromised by inviting

83

back the three chiefs and their families. The invitation was well received. The bulk of the Eskimoes settled down quite happily on the rim of the cwm, while the chiefs and their women and children piled into one of the sledges and followed me down to the igloo. There we offered them caribou cuts (which I could see they took only out of politeness) and colored beads (a number of which Ross had unearthed from the bottom of the sledge and which they accepted with obvious delight). Then, while the children crowded round Somerville to watch him taking snuff, and the women pawed through our possessions with uninhibited interest, I began to question the chief. If only, I thought, I can get him to talk!

"Do your tribe live on the island?" I asked him.

He shook his head.

"Yet you are here now?"

"We have been following the caribou." He gestured to the pathway of trampled snow which ran down like an avalanche weal from the crest of the cwm.

I nodded. That was logical enough.

"It was lucky you found them," I said, "or your tribe would have starved." .

He shrugged.

"Perhaps."

"Or is there," I asked, "something else on the island you might have eaten?"

He shifted uneasily.

"I have heard," I went on, "that there are whales on the shore of this island. Perhaps you would have eaten them?"

His eyes flickered in sudden fear.

"No!" he whispered. "No!"

"But there are whales," I persisted. "And you know where they are."

He shrank back, his eyes wide with terror.

"No," he gasped. "Taboo."

I cursed myself for my impatience. It ought to have occurred to me that there was likely to be a taboo[1] on the graveyard of the whales.

[1] I ought perhaps to explain that an Eskimo's whole life is governed by tribal taboos. These differ from one area to another; but they are all equally binding, and the average Eskimo no more thinks of breaking a taboo than the average white man thinks of committing murder. K. R.

"I meant no harm," I said quickly. "Tell me one thing, and I will never mention the dead whales again. Tell me where I can find them."

Again the chief's eyes widened. He barked an order, and the other two men came hurrying across to him. For some minutes the three of them whispered together, every now and then darting furtive and outraged glances in my direction, until I felt like the little man in a Bateman drawing. The whispering grew more vehement, more impassioned. Then at last the chief drew himself up.

"Because you are a stranger," he said, "we forgive you for breaking the taboo. But you must not mention these things again." He paused, then pointed south (in the direction we had come from). "To find the Lost Ones," he said, "You must travel that way. Towards the melting ice."

I could see he was misdirecting me. It stuck out a mile, but I saw no point in letting on that I didn't believe him.

"Thank you," I said humbly, "and now I have one more question to ask."

He looked at me apprehensively.

"Have you ever," I asked him, "seen another man like ourselves, a man with white skin?"

He shook his head.

"Many months ago," I said, "I believe that such a man came to this island. He came in a great machine which flew through the air like a bird. Have you heard of such a man?"

"No indeed."

And this time, I could see, he was telling the truth. I turned to Ross, who had been listening anxiously.

"He's heard of the whales all right," I translated. "But he's not heard of your son."

Ross's voice was excited. "Find the whales," he whispered, "and we'll find Donald. Ask him where they are."

That, of course, was just what I wanted to do, but couldn't. I was racking my brains for some way of getting round the taboo, when—sudden and unexpected—a woman screamed.

A scream of pain is unnerving enough; but this was worse. It was a scream of terror: unbearable, hysterical terror. Again and again it rang out, echoing and re-echoing round the cwm. I spun round, and saw in a flash what had happened. One of the Eskimo women, nosing among

85

our possessions, had unearthed the whalebone arrows. She stood there, the arrows at her feet, her eyes screwed tight as frosted rosebuds, screaming her head off. Then one of the children—a little boy of about six—also saw the arrows. He clapped a hand over his eyes, and with a piercing howl buried his face in his mother's lap. The chief saw what they were looking at. His eyes widened. He gave a queer half-choking gasp and lurched unsteadily as though his knees had suddenly given way under him; then, pulling himself together, he gasped out an order. And the Eskimoes, their faces averted, began to scramble into their sledge.

They were going. And I knew that nothing I did or said would hold them back.

I cursed myself for not having hidden the arrows—I might have guessed that anything to do with the men with yellow hair would scare an ordinary Eskimo stiff. In a flurry of snow the sledge shot up the cwm as if pursued by the hounds of hell. There was a bedlam of shouting; a great cracking of whips; and the whole tribe fled. Without as much as a backward glance they went streaming away: and suddenly, once again, the cwm lay bare and silent under the moon.

I walked across to the arrows, broke them and trod them into the snow. It was, of course, shutting the door after the horse had bolted, but at least I felt better once they were out of sight.

Well, what had been done couldn't be undone. The Eskimoes had gone, and nothing, I knew, would bring them back. We drew up the Primus, boiled water, and, over our breakfast of cocoa and caribou cuts, I gave the others the gist of my talk with the chief.

"At least," I ended, "we've confirmation of one thing. The graveyard really exists. When I mentioned whales, the Eskimoes were scared to death."

"And," Somerville added grimly, "we've confirmation of something else. The men with yellow hair exist too. When the Eskimoes saw their arrows, they were scared to death of *them!*"

The next few days passed uneventfully. Now that we had plenty of food, our strength and energy soon returned; nor was it long before Ross's snow-blindness cleared up completely (snow-blindness is caused more by physical deterioration than by actual damage to the eyes). Indeed, our physical condition improved so rapidly that the others, I think, would have liked to push on after a rest of only three or four days. But I insisted we lay up for a full week. Sledging north of 75 degrees is no job for the half-fit; and there was no telling what dangers and hardships might lie ahead.

September 28 was the day we at last struck camp and headed up-valley. It was a fine but bitterly cold morning, with a touch of autumn in the fresh north-easterly breeze; and all of us, including the dogs, were glad to keep on the move. We had no difficulty in seeing which way the herd had gone: a hundred thousand caribou leave in their wake a trail of devastation. And we sledged up-valley, following the edge of the riband of tramped-down snow.

At first we took things easily, afraid that the days of near-starvation might have taken their toll; but we needn't have worried—our rest had done us good, and we suffered no repercussions. We also took the most elaborate precautions against our friends with yellow hair. By day we kept close together, our guns at the ready; we chose our route carefully, avoiding dead ground; and when we halted for meals we threw up a snow wall and kept a constant lookout. While each night we picked a camp site that was easy to defend and well out of range of any possible avalanche. These precautions slowed us down. But we deemed them necessary: very necessary. For as soon as we got under way we were plagued by the old familiar feeling of being spied on; and the farther we progressed up-valley the stronger the feeling became. There was, however, nothing we could do about it. We could only push on, keeping our eyes skinned and taking no risks.

Mile after mile we followed the caribou trail as it went winding inland along the floor of the valley. For some time the snow was pleasant for sledging, the valley wide and the gradient easy. But on the morning of the third day (by which time we had covered some fifty miles and were more than half-way across the island), the hills on either side of the valley began to close in and the gradient to steepen. Soon we were hauling the sledge up snow-slopes one in ten—no easy job with only five huskies and the temperature down to minus twenty. We covered less than ten miles that day, and in the evening, having rounded a bend in the upper reaches of the valley, camped with a magnificent but somewhat frightening vista opening out ahead.

Some dozen miles from where we set up the Meade tent, the valley petered out on the fringe of a vast semicircular snow-field. This snow-field itself looked a formidable barrier, but more formidable still was the chain of cliffs lining its farther rim: a thrust-up conglomeration of volcanic rocks, wreathed in cloud, which seemed pretty effectively to bar the way ahead. And yet the caribou trail wound on: over the snow-field: toward the cliffs.

Ross looked at the trampled snow.

"Where the caribou can lead," he said, "we can follow."

I caught Somerville's eye and smiled. The captain was like a bloodhound: having got his nose to the scent, he'd no intention of being put off.

I say that the rocks were "wreathed in cloud" because that was our first impression. But later in the evening, as we sat outside the Meade tent, we had second thoughts. For nowhere else was there a cloud in the sky; and now that we could study it at leisure we could see the opaqueness round the cliffs lay in peculiar two-dimensional layers —a formation more usual to mist than cloud.

How I longed for our binoculars!—now at the bottom of Mould Bay. Without them it was impossible to tell, with any certainty, what problems the morrow would hold. But —cloud or mist—it seemed to me that the future looked pretty forbidding.

Soon after sunrise next morning (which was at a more normal hour, now that we were getting into autumn) we struck camp and headed towards the snow-field. The caribou trail was easy to follow: a flattened pathway over a hundred yards wide. We kept to its fringe, where we had a good view and the going was reasonably smooth; and by midday the trail had led us out of the valley and into the great expanse of virgin snow. We toiled across it, hour after hour, like ants traversing the bowl of an amphitheater. To start with, we were troubled with lassitude, and the glare of the sun was distinctly uncomfortable; but as we approached the cliffs, drifting eddies of mist (so our second thoughts had been right) began to screen off the brightness and to bring us welcome relief. And by five o'clock we were in shadow: the shadow of a line of rugged cliffs which barred our path in a seemingly impassable barrier.

The cliffs were high—a good five hundred feet by my reckoning, and in places close on a thousand; they were sheer; they were a curious ruddy colour, as though they consisted in part of volcanic redstone; and they were shrouded in mist, which pulsated over the top of them, like breath arising from a devil's cauldron.

"Hope they know where they're going!" It was clear from the tone of Somerville's voice that he liked the set-up no better than I did.

We sledged on. Cautiously. As we neared the cliffs, the mist thickened, and visibility dropped. A hundred yards: seventy-five yards: fifty yards.

"*Ai-ee-ee!*"

I hauled the dogs to a halt; and we huddled round the sledge peering suspiciously into the mist like a trio of owls caught in an early sunrise. Of the cliffs there was no sign; they were screened off now by mist; but I knew they couldn't be far ahead.

"I don't fancy this!" I scraped the snow off my skis. And the snow came away wet and unpleasantly cloying.

"If there's a way for the caribou, there's a way for us." This, of course, was Ross.

I shook my head.

"If we go charging in blind, likely as not we'll find ourselves stuck full of arrows, or ground to pulp by an avalanche."

"But we can't stop here!" The captain was indignant.

"We'll not stop," I reassured him, "for long."

I pulled our container of solid fuel off the sledge. The three-by-four-inch bricks of paraffin—designed to fit the Primus—would, I knew, burn well in the open.

"Every fifty yards," I said, "we'll halt the sledge, light one of these, and wait for the heat to disperse the mist."

The others nodded approval; and I set up and lit the first of the fuel bricks. It burned with a clear flame and very little smoke. While waiting for it to take effect, I handed round the Sten guns and rifles.

Well, I can't say that our paraffin brick wholly dispersed the mist, but it definitely thinned it; also, it acted as a marker, in case we wanted to pull back quickly the way we had come.

As soon as the brick was burning freely we resumed our cautious advance, following the caribou trail, and halting every fifty or so yards to light another marker. It was an eerie business. We had just drawn away from the third of our markers when Somerville, who was in the lead, pulled up short.

"Look!" he whispered. "The cliffs!"

Out of the swirling eddies of grey rose a darker more solid outline: reddish-black: the volcanic wall of redstone and shale. We approached it cautiously, guns at the ready, straining our ears to catch the faintest sound. But everything was quiet as death. Nothing moved—excepting the eddies of mist, which rose and fell like restless waves, awash at the solid walls of rock.

We were within fifty yards of the cliffs before we saw the opening: the dark canyon-like defile, with the caribou trail heading towards it, straight as a Russian space missile. We approached it with eager anticipation, and, at its mouth, lit another couple of fuel bricks. But the mist was unusually thick in the defile and refused to be dispersed. We ventured a little way in between the towering walls of rock; but we drew quickly back. For the defile was a place of death: a narrow cleft no more than twenty yards wide, hemmed in by high overhanging cliffs, choked with mist, and with its floor strewn thick with boulders—which had obviously fallen from the cliffs above. Even Ross, I was glad to see, thought discretion the better part of valor; he skittered back to the open with as much alacrity as any of us.

"Whew! What a death-trap!"

We stood in a little circle at the mouth of the defile, wondering what to do next. Try to climb the cliffs? Look for another way through? Call it a day and pitch camp? But always our eyes were drawn back to the opening: back to the billowing folds of mist which lay cotton-wool-like along the defile, bathing the walls of rock in a veneer of glistening damp.

"Maybe the mist thins out farther in."

"And maybe it thickens!"

Ross peered into the gloom, curiosity battling with apprehension.

"What say I take a look? I'll take a light and push on —just a hundred yards."

I didn't like the idea. But I had to admit there was sense in it. It *could* be that the gorge opened out farther in and the mist cleared.

"All right," I said. "But don't go far."

He picked up a brick of paraffin, lit it, and holding it candlewise in front of him advanced into the swirling folds of grey. A dozen paces and he had disappeared. I shifted uneasily.

"What's it like in there?"

His voice came back, muffled and strangely distorted.

"Pretty thick. Can't see a thing!"

"Pretty thick," the cliffs re-echoed. "Can't see a thing!"

A pause, then: "Lot of fallen rock. Cliffs are unstable."

"Don't take any risks," I shouted anxiously.

Another pause: a longer one this time. Then, from surprisingly far away, Ross's voice: suddenly frightened.

"You hear anything?"

Somerville and I stood very still. There was movement all right: all around us: the ever-shifting pattern of mist and glisten of water. But no sound. Or none that we could hear.

"No," I shouted. "But come on back."

What happened next *could* have been an accident: or it could have been caused by our shouting (I knew a young whaler once who could break whole 'bergs off an ice-wall with the ring of his voice). But I don't think it was. For the rock fall had all the split-second timing and precision-placing that spoke of a human hand. Down the cleft the mist turned suddenly black. A whistling roar. And a great deluge of boulders, many of them the size of ten-ton sacks of coal, came hurtling down. Crash! Splatter! Crash! They scythed through the snow and splintered to fragments on the rock beneath. There was a second of shocked silence. Then the professor and I were rushing headlong into the canyon.

"Ross! Ross!"

"Ross! Ross!" The anxious echoes were flung from wall to wall. It seemed impossible that he had escaped being crushed to pulp.

But suddenly, to our relief and amazement, he loomed up in front of us, staggering out of the mist, dazed and shocked, but apparently unhurt. We half-dragged, half-carried him into the open.

91

What had happened he gasped out afterwards—when we were well clear of the treacherous cliffs.

He had, he told us, come to a halt about a hundred yards down the defile and was wondering whether to turn back or push on, when he thought he heard a noise: way up above him. He peered at the cliffs but could see nothing, nothing but the swirling eddies of mist. He told himself he was imagining things, and was about to walk on when he heard the noise again, high up and a little way ahead of where he was standing; it was a noise like the grating together of stones. He thought of the Blond Eskimoes, of the avalanches at Mould Bay; and he felt the hair rise up on the nape of his neck. Carefully he put down the brick of paraffin; he left it, burning brightly, in the middle of the canyon; then he tiptoed quietly across to the left-hand wall, and started to edge his way back. He'd gone no more than a dozen yards before the boulders started to fall: meteor-like, and flush on the candle: flush on the spot where he'd been standing less than ten seconds before. He was drenched with snow, cut and bruised with flying fragments of rock and dazed and shocked with concussion. He heard our shouts; he started to stumble towards us, and a moment later we were hauling him into the open.

We bundled him on to the sledge and shot away from the defile like a posse of scalded tom-cats. We would, in fact, have shot straight out into the snow-field if Somerville hadn't stopped us.

"*Ai-ee-ee!*" While we were still shrouded in mist he hauled the dogs to a halt. "Let's not go into the open."

"Why on earth not?" I leaned on the steering bar, panting.

"If we stay in the mist—out of sight—maybe they'll reckon they got us."

"You think it *was* them?" I looked doubtfully at the cliffs.

"Don't you?"

"Yes," I said slowly. "I reckon it very likely was."

Thinking it out—my mind always worked a good deal slower than the professor's—I could see the point of his stratagem: if the men with yellow hair were watching from the top of the cliffs and saw no sign of us, they might well believe we'd been crushed to death in the defile; and, if that was so, we'd very likely escape their attentions—at least for a while. All the same, I was anxious to put as great a distance as possible between ourselves and the scene of the "accident"; and in the end we hit on the compromise of trying to work our way through the mist, parallel to the line of cliffs. This proved far from easy; but after a while we got the hang of it—heading the dogs in towards the cliffs whenever the mist thinned, and out towards the snow-field whenever it thickened. In this way we pursued a slow and zigzag course until we were a good couple of miles from the defile. Only then did I consider it safe to call a halt.

As soon as the sledge had stopped moving, Ross slid off and began to pace up and down. He seemed more angry than hurt.

"Well! What now?"

"Seems to me," Somerville said quietly, "we've bitten off more than we can chew. I wouldn't be sorry, myself, to head back for Winter Harbour. Next spring we can come again. With proper equipment. *And* a couple of Mounties."

The captain glared at him, outraged.

"You scared of a pack of Eskimoes?"

"These are no ordinary Eskimoes," I cut in. "And we've good reason to be scared of them."

He waved my interruption aside.

"An Eskimo's an Eskimo, whatever color his hair. Damned if I'll give 'em the satisfaction of seeing me run."

There was an awkward silence.

"So you reckon," I said at last, "we ought to push on?"

"Why not? There's bound to be another way over the cliffs."

"All right," I said slowly. "We said we'd give it a fortnight, and so we will. But with this proviso. One more brush with the men with yellow hair, and we head straight for Winter Harbour. We came here to look for whales, not to pick a fight with the Eskimoes."

"And who's picking the fight?"

Ross was indignant. But Somerville, I was glad to see, nodded approval.

Well, that settled our long-term plans; but it didn't settle the immediate question of what to do next. We were, it seemed to me, between the devil and the deep. For it would soon be time to pitch camp; and if we camped in the snow-field the Eskimoes would spot us, and if we camped under the cliffs the Eskimoes would all too likely follow our trail, creep up unobserved in the mist and pepper us full of arrows. Of the two alternatives I definitely preferred the former!

In the end we decided our best plan was to keep on sledging parallel to the cliffs until it was quite dark—by which time we hoped that the Eskimoes (not having seen us) would have gone home for the night assuming us dead. Then we would emerge from the mist and camp in darkness in the open snow-field.

This scheme we followed as well as we could. But by nine o'clock the dogs were utterly exhausted. And so were we. Our progress became slower and slower, our halts, longer and longer, until we finally reached the end of our tether. Whether we were spotted or not we *had* to pitch camp.

In the quiet of the twilight, soon after ten o'clock, we emerged from the mist and struck into the snow-field, hoping the light was uncertain enough to screen us from prying eyes. We set up the Meade tent about two hundred yards from the edge of the mist, built our snow wall, cooked our supper and settled down thankfully for the night.

Or rather two of us settled down for the night. The third kept watch: and very much on the *qui vive*.

We were too exhausted to do much talking, but just before we dropped off to sleep Somerville and I did exchange a few words about the mist. We were rolled up in our sleeping bags; and from where we lay we could see Ross's silhouette through the flap of the tent: a pillar of black delineated sharply against a swirling background of grey. It was the background that puzzled me.

"It's funny"—I spoke more to myself than to Somerville —"It's funny there should be so much mist."

The professor showed signs of interest.

"Why funny?"

"There's usually no mist this far north. Except in mid-summer."

"And why's that?"

"Mist," I said slowly, "is caused by heat. And there's

94

nothing to generate heat in the Arctic—except the mid-summer sun."

Yet the mist was here. Now. It was quite a phenomenon; for it was October, and the sun was near-heatless.

"If the heat doesn't come from the sun," Somerville said thoughtfully, "it must come from something else."

I nodded. That was logical enough.

Well, it was a nice problem all right: the sort, I fancy, that Sherlock Holmes would have enjoyed getting his teeth into. But I was too tired, right then, to puzzle it out. I was still agreeing with Somerville—nodding wisely away—when I fell into a deep exhausted sleep.

In the small hours of the morning, however, I had plenty of opportunity to play Sherlock Holmes; for at 3 a.m. I started my stint as sentry.

It was a fine morning, with moon, aurora and stars giving between them a light that was almost as bright as day; and from where we were camped I could see the cliffs quite clearly. And an imposing sight they were, sweeping in a great symmetrical crescent round the rim of the snow-field. There was something about the light which seemed to accentuate their ruddy colouring; while the mist, ever rising and falling, now laying bare some tower-like promontory, now shrouding it in Stygian gloom, gave the scene a touch of mystery that was more than a little macabre. What was it Somerville and I had agreed about the mist? To have mist you must have heat; this late in the year the heat couldn't come from the sun: it must, therefore, come from something else. But what? I paced up and down, glad to have something to occupy my mind. But the hours passed. And no solution came.

It was the rising sun which gave me the clue I needed. At 5 a.m. it burst like an oriflamme over the rim of the snow-field, bathing the line of cliffs with fingers of fire, accentuating their peculiar redness. And this redness rang a bell. Of course, redstone was volcanic. The hot geysers of Rotorua, the thermal springs of Iceland, the mud pools of Kyushu—half the active volcanic areas in the world were set amid rocks of tertiary redstone—just like the cliffs lining the snow-field.

What more likely, then, than that the heat generating the mist came from volcanoes?

I was elated: proud of myself as a peacock. For the

more I thought my theory over, the more perfectly it fitted. It explained everything. The mist, which had hampered Stefansson, the Air Survey, and now us. The whales, which doubtless drifted inshore where warm water rivers (fed by volcanic springs) broke up the pack ice. The caribou, which doubtless came north to forage for food beside the hot springs. And the men with yellow hair, who no doubt had a village somewhere in the thermal region where, for generations, they had remained undiscovered, hidden by the canopy of mist.

Over breakfast I explained my theory to the others; and they were as sold on it as I was. It was an exciting thought: that on the other side of the cliffs, maybe only a few miles from where we stood, lay the legendary graveyard of the whales, the graveyard which so many people had dreamed of and searched for, and whose secrets we might well be about to lay bare.

We struck camp early, spurred on partly by expectation and partly by a desire to get back into the mist before we were spotted; and by seven o'clock we were heading towards the cliffs. We made straight for a small glacier, which struck us as being the likeliest place for making an ascent—we had already agreed that an ascent was the only answer; for there was no way round the cliffs, and wild horses couldn't have dragged us back to the defile!

We reached the glacier at noon.

It was shrouded in mist; and this made it hard to judge how difficult an ascent would prove. But as far as we could tell it promised to be an easy climb for men, but a difficult haul for huskies and sledge.

And it turned out to be exactly that.

To start with, over the moraine, we made good progress. Then came trouble: the séracs and crevasses of the glacier. We untethered the dogs and let them fend for themselves—which meant, of course, that we had to haul the sledge. One of us would go first, picking a route and kicking steps in the ice (which was mercifully soft); then came the huskies, picking their way surprisingly daintily among the séracs; and last of all came the rearguard—two of us ahaul on the sledge, which seemed to become heavier every minute, to stick in every possible patch of slush and to slide alarmingly towards all the most dangerous crevasses. By ourselves we would probably have climbed the glacier in a couple of hours. With the sledge to haul after us it took us six hours: six hours of unadulterated slogging. It was, I think, the most exhausting day's work I have ever put in—carving up whale carcasses was a sinecure by comparison. But everything, mercifully, comes to an end for those who can stay the course; and a little after seven o'clock that evening we were hauling ourselves and the sledge off the glacier and on to the rocky plateau which lay at the top of the cliffs.

We were too exhausted to contemplate pushing on: too exhausted, even, to take much interest in the strange volcanic world we had clambered into. All we wanted was to find a decent site to pitch camp in, and to settle down for the night. We soon discovered, however, that a decent camp site was impossible to find. For the terrain was highly volcanic—a maze of craters, faults and areas of frightening softness; while over everything lay the mist, veiling the jagged outcrops of rock, gathering in pools of darkness among the craters and faults, hiding any number of dangers—both imagined and real.

After casting about for some time, becoming increasingly exhausted and despondent, we finally came to the rim of a dead volcano which seemed to be reasonably free of mist. Here we set up the tent, with its back to an outcrop of granite and its entrance looking out across the volcano's crater. It was a macabre setting—like the décor for some fantastic ballet from Dante's *Inferno*—and, later in the evening as darkness closed in around us, I noticed something I didn't like: the mist in the crater was rising and thickening. Soon it was coiling, in grey insidious wreaths, right up to the mouth of the tent.

I shivered.

Still, I told myself, there's nothing to be afraid of. The men with yellow hair can hardly have seen us climbing the glacier; and even if they did, we'll be mounting a guard; he'll be carrying a Sten gun; and the dogs will be sleeping beside the tent. And I must admit that as that evening I climbed into my sleeping bag, I had no forebodings, no premonitions of disaster. Perhaps I was too tired. I lay down thankfully, fell asleep at once, and my dreams were untroubled.

It was the light that woke me: the sickly yellow light. For a second I thought I was back aboard the *Northern*

Harvester, and the light was the light of our arc lamp guiding the helicopter in to land. Then I heard a scuffle, a grunt, and a strangled gasp. The flap of the tent was wrenched aside. And there, silhouetted in the glare of their blazing torches, were the men with yellow hair.

9

The Girl with
the "Bewitchen Sent of FlowerS"

I ROLLED to the floor. I made a dive for the Sten gun. But a
foot smashed down on my wrist, and a club—a heavy
whale-bone club—thudded across the back of my neck.

"Do not move, white man."

The voice was expressionless; the dialect was one I
could barely understand. But words weren't needed. The
blow from the club was enough. I lay still.

My first thought was "Why doesn't he kill me and get it
over?" Then, as I noticed Ross and Somerville being
trussed up like a couple of chickens, hope came surging
back. For we weren't, it seemed, going to be killed at all
—at least, not for the moment: we were going to be made
prisoner. I started to take things in then; and when a man
knows his life is hanging in the balance, he takes things in
pretty quickly.

Our captors numbered about a dozen. They were small,
wiry men, with blond shoulder-length hair, and a far paler
skin than the average Eskimo (due, we decided afterwards, to their spending so much of their lives in perpetual mist). They were dressed in the usual Eskimo clothes:
loose-fitting jerkins and trousers of hide or fur, with knee-

high boots of sealskin. A few of them carried stout, very flexible bows—which looked as though they were made from strips of baleen; the rest, clubs. They were tough-looking customers. They were also—strange as it sounds—Nordic looking; and this struck me as being even more surprising than their blond hair and archaic weapons; for all the Eskimoes I'd ever come across had been of Polynesian or Mongolian stock—having broad noses, flat features and almond eyes; yet the features of the men with yellow hair were almost classical Scandinavian!

We weren't, however, given much opportunity to puzzle this out. For our captors were in a hurry. They trussed us up—the fellow who secured me tied knots like a bos'n—then, quickly and efficiently, they dismantled the tent, loaded the stores and sorted out the huskies. As soon as they were ready to move off, the largest of them (who seemed to be some sort of chief) pointed first at me then at our sledge.

"Climb in, white man."

I pretended not to cotton on—for I didn't want it known that I understood their language. He gave an exasperated grunt, picked me up as though I'd been a bale of hay, and dumped me on top of our stock of caribou cuts. Ross and Somerville were heaved into place beside me. Then, with a great cracking of whips, the sledges shot forward into the mist. And for some time we were too frightened to speak.

For the dogs ran fast, charging flat-out into the swirling curtain of grey. How the drivers knew where they were going I can't imagine; but somehow we managed to miss the chasms, the craters and the outcrops of rock; and I could only suppose that the Eskimoes knew the terrain so well that they could have sledged it blindfold. We huddled together, partly to keep warm, partly to take stock of our predicament.

"What do you reckon they'll do with us?" Ross was apprehensive.

"Looks," I said, "as if they're taking us back to their village."

"If they'd been going to kill us, they'd have finished us off in the tent, wouldn't they?"

I said nothing. I couldn't help remembering that they had tried to kill us twice before.

While the sledge swayed drunkenly through a world of shifting grey, we weighed the odds of escape. They were pretty slim. We might, it is true, have managed to roll off the sledge; but where would that get us? The Blond Eskimoes could obviously see in the mist far better than we could; and even if by some miracle we managed to avoid recapture, we would (without dogs, arms or stoves) very soon die of exposure. We thought of making a grab for our guns; but we were trussed up like chickens, and the guns were at the far end of the sledge. In the end we agreed that, apart from trying to work loose the leather straps that bound us, there was nothing we could do. We would have to wait on events.

On we sledged, hour after jolting hour; until at last the eastern sky turned gold, and the heat of a rising sun began to suck away the worst of the mist. Only then could we see something of the country through which we were sledging. And what fantastic country it was!

In every direction, as far as the eye could see, there stretched a series of great volcanic plateaus, intersected by sheer rifts (many of them almost a hundred feet in depth). The rocks of the plateaus—magma, sulphur and basalt—glowed red and yellow and pearly-grey; while the beds of the rifts were strung, necklace-like, with countless craters and lakes. I noticed that in one of the latter slender columns of spray were pulsating up, like the blows from a pod of whales. I pointed them out to Somerville.

"Your hot springs," he said.

And I nodded.

Not long after this we heard, away in the distance, the howl of huskies; and a few minutes later, debouching out of a ravine, we saw our goal about half a mile ahead: a largish village rising steeply in terraces on the farther shore of a lake.

Now it would be meaningless for me to say that the village in front of us didn't look like a typical Eskimo village: because a typical Eskimo village, as such, simply doesn't exist. There's no conformity in the Arctic: in Greenland, for example, the Eskimoes build their houses of stone and earth, in the Coronation Gulf of snow-blocks, in the Mackenzie Delta of driftwood and reed, and in Alaska of circles of turf (sod huts they're usually called). But I can say this: the settlement we were now approaching looked like no other Eskimo village that I'd seen or heard of in all my thirty years in the Arctic. It had, for one thing, obviously been laid out with an eye to defense; and since Eskimoes never fight each other, defensibility is something they normally don't give a thought to. For another thing, it had a decidedly permanent look; whereas most Eskimo settlements are a temporary home only, abandoned each year as the tribe moves on to fresh hunting grounds. Again, the houses in this village were of different sizes—indicating, it seemed to me—their owners' different status; whereas in the normal Eskimo settlement the houses are identical—symbols of a way of life that is strictly Communistic in outlook. All this we could see at a glance, as we approached the village down a gentle incline which terminated in a broad riband of water: a freshwater lake which served as the settlement's first line of defense. Across the riband of water, which we were now approaching at a fast gallop, there ran a causeway. This was blocked at its farther end by a stockade, high and strong, and built out of something which looked from a distance like planks of bleached wood. Immediately behind the stockade was a strip of narrow ground, filled with square, substantial-looking huts. Then the hill rose steeply, in terrace after terrace, each filled with buildings and connected to the level above it by ladders (which could obviously, if need be, be drawn up). The general impression was one of a permanent settlement which could, at a moment's notice, turn itself into a near-impregnable fortress.

Soon we were pelting down the causeway and approaching the stockade which ran without a break, as far as I could see, across our path. There seemed to be no way through; but as we neared it, the big Eskimo, who was in charge of us, gave a curious hooting whistle; and at once a gateway swung open.

As we passed through, I let out a gasp of amazement. For I saw that the stockade wasn't, as I had thought at first, built of wood. It was built of whalebone: great curving ribs of whalebone, which formed a solid wall at least thirty feet high.

But before the implications of this had sunk home, we were galloping into the village itself.

A good number of people were bustling about. All of them, I noticed, had fair hair and the same curiously Nordic features as the men who had taken us prisoner. As our sledge careered past, they stared at us in obvious astonishment. We sat up and tried to look dignified and unconcerned: no easy job with our wrists tied firmly behind our backs and our minds (to say the least) decidedly apprehensive. For something like a hundred yards we sledged along a clearly defined road, then pulled up with a flourish in front of one of the larger huts.

"Inside, white men."

The big Eskimo pointed to the hut.

It was obvious what he wanted. There was no point in pretending we didn't understand; especially as a crowd was beginning to assemble, and we had no wish to be publicly hoisted off the sledge like so many sacks of potatoes. We clambered down and followed the Eskimo into the hut.

It was a solid building, about twelve feet square, made of turves bound together with a sort of tarry substance (which I later discovered was a mixture of asphalt and sulphur skimmed off the near-by springs; and with a roof of reeds, laid neatly into a weatherproof thatch. I quite expected to find a committee of reception inside; but the hut was empty—devoid of people, furniture or any sort of ornament. There was simply the stamped-down earth of the floor, the reed-covered roof and the turf walls—broken by a doorway and a single glassless window, which let in both light and cold. Here we were left.

Our first step, of course, was to examine the door and the window; but outside both a pair of Eskimoes had been left on guard. We looked at their great whalebone clubs, decided that discretion was the better part of valor, and agreed to restrict our activity to trying to loosen each other's bonds.

Now I know that in all the best adventure stories people who are tied up invariably manage to work themselves free. But we, alas, didn't seem to have the knack! Apart from anything else, we had been tied with leather thongs, which had been first wetted in the snow; and I doubt if anything short of a razor blade would have made much impression on them. We scratched away until our nails were broken and our fingers numb; we rubbed against the walls of the hut (there weren't any convenient sharp-edged stones) until our wrists were chafed and bleeding; we jerked and twisted and levered until we were quite exhausted. But we made not the slightest impression.

Eventually, tired and dispirited, we gave up and squatted down in front of the window. From here we at least had a first-class view of the crowd which was assembling in the square of level ground in front of the hut. As far as we could make out they were more curious than hostile.

After some time I realized I was hungry—it was getting on for midday now, and we hadn't eaten since the previous evening.

"I'll try asking for food," I said to the others. "It can't do any harm."

"In Eskimo?" Somerville sounded doubtful.

I shook my head.

"We'll keep that one up our sleeve," I said.

I pushed my head through the window and whistled; and one of the guards, swinging his club, came across.

"We want food," I said in English. And I pointed to my mouth and champed my jaws like an impatient horse.

He nodded, waved his hand towards a hut on the far side of the square, and a second later a young boy, whom I took to be some sort of messenger, came pushing through the crowd.

"The white men want food," I heard the guard say to him. "Are they allowed any?"

"I will see."

The boy disappeared for about ten minutes; then came pushing his way back.

"Yes," I heard him say, "Freyja will bring food. You can untie the men while they eat, then tie them up again."

I translated this to the others, adding that if our captors were going to give us food they had, presumably, forgotten their amiable intention of killing us—at least for the time being! After a deal of discussion we agreed that as soon as we had been untied and had eaten, I should demand, in Eskimo, to see the tribal chief. We reasoned that with any luck our captors would be surprised at finding we spoke their language, and that we'd be able to talk ourselves out of trouble.

"And you might," Ross added, "ask them about my son. He could be here. Right in the village."

We took it in turns to watch through the window; and

after about half an hour I spotted a girl, carrying a large bowl, pushing her way through the crowd.

"Here comes Freyja," I said.

Somerville, joining me at the window, let out a most unprofessor-like whistle.

"Looks more like a movie star!" he said.

The captain joined us.

"Let's hope," he grunted, "she can cook!"

One of our guards entered the hut. He cut off our bonds, then beckoned to the girl, who was waiting outside the doorway, and she came in.

She was slim, fair-haired and beautiful; so beautiful, in fact, that we could only stare at her in astonished silence —much, I fancy, as the Trojans of old must have gazed at Helen as she walked the walls of Troy. She took not the slightest notice of us, but walked to the middle of the hut and put down the bowl. Then as she turned to leave, she caught sight of Ross out of the corner of her eye. She spun round; her hand flew to her mouth; and she stared at him with a sort of incredulous intensity. She took a step towards him. We thought she was going to speak. Then the shadow of the guard fell across the doorway; and, seeing it, she licked her lips, turned and walked slowly out of the hut.

"I will come to collect the bowl," I heard her say, "when the white men have finished."

The guard laughed and said something I didn't catch. The girl shrugged, and a second later she was lost in the crowd.

"Phew!" muttered Ross. "And did you notice her perfume?"

I nodded.

"The girl with the 'bewitchen sent of flowers,'" I said. "I also noticed," I added, "that you seemed to make quite an impression on the lady!"

Ross looked vaguely sheepish, and Somerville laughed.

"You know what sailors are!" he said.

But though we joked, we were puzzled. We settled down to our food in silence, thinking over this new and totally unexpected development. The food was hot and appetizing: a mixture of whale meat, caribou and some sort of lichen: and we tucked in with a will.

"She'll be back soon," I said, "for the bowl."

"Let's eat slowly," Somerville suggested. "If we've food left, it'll give her a chance to stay and talk."

It seemed a reasonable idea—for the girl had certainly looked as if she had wanted to say something. We forced ourselves to eat slowly.

"Should I speak to her in Eskimo?" I said after awhile.

We were still debating this, and the prospect of getting her to help us escape, when we saw the girl again pushing her way towards the hut. She paused by the doorway, spoke for a few seconds to one of the guards, then she came in: nervously, with a sort of suppressed excitement.

She walked straight up to Ross. She stared at him very intently. Then, pointing to the sky, she said—slowly and distinctly, as though wanting to be quite certain he understood—"Helicopter?"

We caught our breath, as the significance of the single word struck home. Ross's face lit up. I have never seen a man so transformed in a single moment. He grabbed my arm.

"She's seen Donald. Ask where he is."

"Where," I said to the girl (speaking in Eskimo) "is the man who came in the helicopter?"

She caught her breath—obviously surprised at my speaking her language—then she turned to me eagerly.

"Who is that man?" She pointed to Ross.

"He is the father," I said, "of the man who came in the helicopter."

"What does he want?"

"He wants to find his son. Do you know where he is?"

"Last spring," she said, "Donald went to search for the Lost Ones." Her eyes clouded, and she began to twist and untwist her hands. "Now," she half-whispered, "I fear he is dead."

"Tell us about him. Quickly."

She glanced nervously at the doorway. "Over a year ago," she whispered, "he came flying through the air like a great bird. He had been caught in a storm, and his helicopter was damaged. Close to the village he tumbled out of the sky, breaking the helicopter and hurting his leg. Our men found him and brought him back, and because —like us—he had fair hair he was allowed to live. He lived with us happily: very happily: until"—her voice broke—"he went to search for the Lost Ones."

106

All this I translated to Ross.

"I knew it!" His eyes were shining. "He's alive. *And* we're going to find him. Ask her what are these Lost Ones he went to search for."

The girl licked her lips.

"The Lost Ones," she whispered, "are the whales. The dead whales."

"And where are they?"

Her eyes were frightened, and I thought at first she wasn't going to answer; but eventually she half-whispered:

"They are inside the mouth of hell."

We were obviously terrifying her. And no wonder, I thought, seeing that the graveyard was not only taboo but was also—apparently—inside the mouth of the Eskimo hell. I decided to change the subject.

"Why," I asked, "have your men bound us?"

"You should not have come," she said. "You ignored our warnings, and now you must pay."

"But why shouldn't we have come? We wish your people no harm."

"You are like the others. Even Donald. All you want is the magic stone."

It was my turn to start getting excited now.

"You mean the stone inside the Lost Ones? The stone that makes the scent?"

She nodded. "But you will never get it," she said. "The stone is ours. Those who come to steal it, die. You, too, will die," she added matter-of-factly, "tonight."

My throat went suddenly dry.

"What's the matter?" Somerville asked quickly.

"She says we're going to be killed. Tonight."

There was a long silence; then the professor said quietly:

"Tell her that if we're killed we won't be able to help her look for Donald."

Somerville, I realized then, had seen things much more acutely than either Ross and I. Ross had been obsessed with the thought of finding his son; I had been obsessed with the thought of finding the ambergris. As a result neither of us had grasped the full significance of all the girl had been saying. As soon as I translated Somerville's remark I saw what I had previously missed.

Freyja's eyes lit up: she clasped her hands in delight.

"You will help me find him?"

For a moment her joy was unbounded. Then the sparkle gave way to doubt.

"But no. He is dead. Why else has he not come back to me?"

It was no time for half measures.

"He is alive," I said. "We know he is alive. Help us escape, and we'll find him together."

She looked at me doubtfully.

"You are not afraid? You will go past the guardians: into the mouth of hell?"

"We are not afraid," I said.

She looked from one to the other of us.

"I believe you," she said at last.

"Then you'll help us escape?"

In the distance a drum started to throb softly, persistently. The crowd stirred, and I could sense their mounting excitement.

Freyja crossed to the window. When she saw what was happening her voice was anxious.

"It is Loki."

"Who on earth's Loki?"

"The Shaman. He has come to judge you."

"Tell us what happens. Quickly."

"This evening," she said, "there will be music and feasting. You will be brought to the shore of the lake. Then Loki will climb to the rock of judgment and fling his staff into the water. If it drifts to the right you will be set free. If it drifts to the left you will be killed."

"Perhaps," I said hopefully, "it will drift to the right."

But she shook her head.

"Always," she said, "he flings it to where the currents flow left."

The crowd murmured with excitement. There was a shouting of orders: running footsteps: and a guard looked in through the doorway.

"Leave the white men, Freyja," he ordered. "Loki is here."

I cursed.

The girl picked up the bowl.

"Whatever happens," she whispered, "You won't be killed until dawn."

"Listen!" I grabbed her by the arm. I spoke quickly. Urgently. "This is what you must do . . ."

I was still whispering instructions, when there came an angry bellow from the guard.

"Freyja!"

And with a half-frightened, half-reassuring smile she was gone.

I could only hope she had understood what I'd told her to do.

We moved across to the window, and watched the yellow-haired Eskimoes forming themselves into a sort of procession. For some minutes they milled about in apparent confusion, then they went streaming away in the wake of a sledge—which we assumed was the Shaman's—and soon the square was deserted, except for our guards.

I told the others exactly what the girl and I had been saying. One thing was clear: we were in trouble, serious trouble; and I can't say I fancied our chances of getting out of it. Indeed, the more I thought things over, the more convinced I became that we had only one hope, only one single straw at which we could clutch. The girl. I said as much to the others. Somerville nodded; but Ross's reaction was different. He started to pace the hut.

"I don't trust her," he burst out at last.

"Why ever not?" Somerville was surprised.

"Why *should* she want to help us find Donald?"

"I'd have thought that was obvious!" I said.

The captain grunted, sheering away from something he obviously didn't like. "All right," he said at last, "but if she wanted to find him, why didn't she go before? By herself?"

"She's probably been afraid to," I said.

"Afraid? Afraid of what?"

"Of going near the graveyard, I suppose. Remember it's taboo. *And,* apparently, inside the mouth of hell."

Ross looked unconvinced.

"That seems a fair enough reason to me," Somerville put in. "After all, the girl is an Eskimo."

"An Eskimo!"

The captain's face darkened, and he resumed his pacing, up and down the hut.

As I looked at him in some astonishment, my eye met

Somerville's, and he—I could tell—was as puzzled as I was.

Our exchange of looks wasn't lost on the captain.

"I'm sorry," his voice was half-angry, half-defensive, "but he is my son, you know!"

Well, we'd enough on our plates, it seemed to me, without getting involved in a tiff on racial discrimination. So I steered the conversation round to something practical; a plan of escape. All afternoon and half the evening we worked on scheme after scheme; although we all felt, I think, that none of them had very much chance of success. By sunset we had talked ourselves to exhaustion; and one by one, worn out with strain and apprehension, we drifted into an uneasy sleep. But sleep didn't bring an end to our fears. Our dreams were troubled. On the stamped-down earth of the hut we twisted and turned like a trio of string-jerked marionettes. For the second time in as many weeks there seemed every prospect of our expedition coming to a sticky end.

10

Escape

It was the drumming that woke us: soft and monotonous, its tempo never rising, never falling.

I got up and looked out of the window. The night was dark, with the moon not yet risen and drifting layers of mist obscuring the stars. The village seemed to be strangely deserted, and I soon saw why. Down by the lake a great procession was forming up: fair-haired Eskimoes by the hundred, men, women and children, each of them carrying a flaming resinous torch.

The others joined me at the window, and together we watched the procession as it moved slowly along the shore.

"Looks like the start of the trial," Somerville grunted.

I nodded.

As we stood watching, filled with misgiving but not being able to do anything about it, a sledge swept into the square and pulled up outside the door of our hut. Off it jumped five or six Eskimoes, including the big fellow who had been in charge of the party that captured us. He saw us peering through the window, and jerked his thumb at the sledge.

"Climb on, white men."

We were in no position to argue.

As we sledged through the deserted village we kept our

eyes open for the chance of escape. But none presented itself—our hands were tied and the guards watched us
closely. Soon we were clear of the houses and sledging
parallel to the shore of the lake: on one side of us, the
steeply rising hillside dotted with torch-carrying Eskimoes;
on the other, the water ashimmer with the reflected light
from countless flares. Three or four hundred yards beyond
the village we came to a small rocky eminence, backed by
sheer cliffs and jutting platform-like into the lake. Here we
halted.

"Off the sledge, white men."

We climbed down, and peered anxiously about us. The
platform on which we had been dumped like so many
sacks of potatoes, was quite small, about twenty yards
square I'd say; and on three sides it was lined by a double
row of Eskimoes, drawn up like a guard of honor—or
was it like the guard surrounding a scaffold? I shivered,
and the others, evidently, felt as I did.

"Don't fancy this!" Somerville whispered.

Neither did I. And yet, I thought, they can hardly be
going to finish us off before the trial and even if the trial
goes against us, didn't the girl say we'd be safe till sunrise?

We huddled nervously together, while above and behind
us the torch-carrying procession wound its way along zigzag terraces cut into the cliffs. Up and up the procession
climbed, until at last the whole of the cliff face from lake
to summit was threaded with a spiral staircase of light.
Once the Eskimoes were all in position, the drum-beat,
which up to now had been slow and muted, began to
quicken. It became gradually louder, gradually harsher,
and gradually more abandoned; the torches began to bob
up and down, and after awhile we became aware of a
quick rhythmic chanting—"Loki, Loki, Loki" it sounded
like—keeping time to the throb of the drums. As the
drumming swelled to a crescendo, so the chanting rose to
a frenetic high-pitched howl; for a second both combined
in a tumultuous ear-splitting climax, then they stopped:
stopped dead, as an orchestra in full flood stops at the
drop of a conductor's baton; and simultaneously every
torch was extinguished. It was as though some giant hand
had spread in an instant across the face of the cliff . . .
Silence, and darkness, and the drifting patches of mist
. . . Then on the very top of the cliffs, immediately above

our platform, a single light flared out like a beacon; and in its glare a man stood silhouetted against the skyline. I guessed it was Loki, the Shaman. For a full minute he stood motionless, his outline etched in fire, the one fragment of color in a world of Stygian black. Suddenly, dramatically, he raised what looked like a staff high over his head; then in a great spinning arc he flung it into the lake.

As the staff hit the water immediately in front of our platform, the torches were rekindled—as suddenly and instantly as they had been doused—and the Eskimoes thronged to the edge of the terraces to watch. We scurried across the platform—to the side fronting the lake, which was free of guards.

"Which way," muttered Ross, "is it going?"

Now that the staff was in the water we had difficulty in spotting it; but eventually I picked it up, a fragment of flotsam tugged hither and thither by the underwater currents.

"Right," I said. "Thank God for that."

But it was too good to be true. For a few seconds the staff did indeed edge to the right. Then it came to a stop; uncertainly it twisted and turned, plucked at by random eddies; then once again it started to move; slowly at first, then, as it came into the grip of a steady current, with gathering momentum. And this time it moved to the left. On and on it drifted, steadily, inexorably farther and farther left; past the platform; past the village; soon it was out of sight.

The sign was unmistakable. The gods had spoken.

A low hissing sigh rose from the terraces, and the torches bobbed up and down as the Eskimoes wound their way back to the village. The "trial" was over.

Our guards' attitude took a change for the worse. They were openly hostile now. They grabbed hold of us. They manhandled us back to the sledge. Ross, who was rash enough to show fight, got his legs knocked from under him and fell heavily, face down in the snow. He picked himself up muttering angrily.

"For heaven's sake," I hissed, "take it easy."

And much to my relief he subsided on to the sledge-boards, more shaken I think, than he cared to admit.

We were driven back to the village and bundled, none to gently, into the same hut as before. The straps binding our wrists were checked and tightened. And then we were left.

Once alone, we looked at each other in silence: and the fear we had so far managed to keep in check swept over us: suddenly unleashed: like flood-water bursting through the walls of a damn.

I walked across to the window—if I looked as frightened as the others, I didn't want them to see me. Looking out, I noticed our guard had been doubled. Four Eskimoes now were patrolling outside the hut, and another four—the reserves—were pacing the square.

"They don't mean," I said, "to take any chances."

Somerville screwed himself round like a contortionist and peered at his watch. He was, I think, the most composed of the three of us.

"Twelve o'clock," he said. "We've six hours till dawn. A lot can happen in six hours."

He was putting his trust, I could tell, in the girl.

We sat on the floor of the hut: waiting, hoping. There was nothing else we could do. Time passed slowly.

A sudden commotion, a sudden burst of talk, and out of the darkness came some half-dozen Eskimoes, dragging behind them our huskies, sledge and stores. These they proceeded to pile up, higgledy-piggledy against the wall of our hut. Ross's eyes widened in sudden interest.

"What's the idea?" he grunted. "They trying to make it easy for us?"

Now I knew very well what the idea was, and I tried to change the subject. But Ross wouldn't have it. He must be put in the picture; and at last I was obliged to tell him.

"If you must know," I said, "it's a nice old Eskimo custom that when a stranger dies in another tribe's territory, he isn't buried alone; his possessions are buried with him."

In the silence that followed I looked at the hands of Somerville's watch: 1:15. Less than five hours to dawn.

Time dragged. We didn't, of course, sleep. We talked, walked up and down to stop ourselves getting cramp, and went on trying to work loose our bonds—but without the slightest hint of success. After awhile we fell to discussing what looked like being our last card: if the girl failed us, I'd make a last-minute demand, in Eskimo, to see the Shaman. The hands of Somerville's watch crawled round and

114

round and round again; slowly; inexorably: 3 a.m., 4 a.m., 5 a.m.

"She's not coming," I said at last.

"Told you I didn't trust her." Ross's voice was bitter.

But Somerville still kept hope.

"She'll come," he said.

Five-thirty A.M. And footsteps, quick and light, echoing among the huts. And a girl's voice, arguing with the guards.

"It's Freyja," I whispered.

We could tell she was having trouble in getting through.

We waited in an agony of hope. We didn't dare look out of the window. We could only sit and listen and pray. And our prayers were answered. The door swung open and Freyja, carrying a bowl and a candle, came softly into the hut. She crossed to where we were sitting, huddled against the wall.

"Have you got them?" I whispered.

She nodded.

Kneeling down she placed bowl and candle on the floor, and at the same time split out of her dress about a dozen cylindrical tubes.

"I can't stay," she whispered.

And almost before we'd woken up to the fact that she had come, she was slipping noiselessly out of the hut.

"Quick!" I hissed. "The knife!"

Thank God it was there. Ross hoiked it out from the bottom of the bowl, and Somerville scratched away at the wall and hid it behind a couple of loose reeds. While the others dealt with the knife, I scoured out three grooves in the earth, and started to bury the cylindrical tubes; the last of our sticks of dynamite. We worked quickly—terrified that any moment a guard might look in through the door —and in less time than it takes to describe, we were smoothing down the earth, wedging more reeds in front of the knife, and covering up our tracks. Then we waited. Impatiently.

Twenty minutes later, when the guard came to collect bowl and candle, our food had been eaten and we were apparently fast asleep. And it was just as well we hadn't tried anything clever. For the guard was suspicious. He hauled us to our feet, checked our bonds and peered and prodded around the hut. I thought for one terrible moment that he had spotted the loose reeds in front of the knife, but at last he gave a satisfied grunt, picked up bowl and candle, and stalked out. The time was coming up to six o'clock.

"Hurry," Ross muttered. "We've less than an hour."

He unearthed the knife, and started to saw away at the strap binding my wrists. With his own hands firmly tied it wasn't easy. It took ten minutes of painful fumbling sawing before the leather parted. But once I was free I made short work of releasing the others. For several minutes we crouched there in silence, flexing and massaging our wrists, and hopping from foot to foot as the blood rushed back to our dead-white fingers in a tingling, agonizing flood. Then, moving very quietly, I handed round the sticks of dynamite. We didn't talk much; we had made our plans beforehand; but Ross did raise one point.

"Where," he whispered, "are we picking up the girl?"

"On the way to the stockade," I told him.

"I suppose we *have* to take her?"

"Of course." Somerville's voice was sharp.

The captain, I could see, wasn't pleased.

"Come on," I muttered. "First things first. We're not out of the hut yet."

Very carefully I inserted two of the sticks of dynamite into the base of the wall. As I lit the fuses my hands were trembling. We scurried to the opposite side of the hut. We lay face-down on the floor, forearms over our heads. Five seconds: ten seconds: fifteen seconds: perhaps the fuses were damp? Then, near-simultaneous, two shattering explosions. The wall disintegrated—a hole some six feet square being blown completely out; the roof collapsed; the reeds caught fire, and through the smoke, the flames and the falling debris we rushed headlong into the night.

One of the guards lay flat on his face, stunned. One had taken to his heels—I saw him disappearing across the square. But the other two, clubs at the ready, were coming fast round the hut. A stick of dynamite landed flush in their path. It exploded straight under their feet; it flung them aside like a pair of string-jerked puppets—and they lay still, whether dead or stunned we didn't have time to find out. I pulled out my knife and hacked at the guy ropes which tethered the sledge. Queequeg and the rest of the huskies were howling their heads off. And every dog in the village seemed to be answering. All was bedlam and confusion; and a group of Eskimoes, several of them armed with bows, came streaming out of a hut on the opposite side of the square.

"Quick!" I gasped. "The Sten gun."

It was no time to be squeamish. Already one arrow had hummed past my ear, and another had pinned Somerville to the sledge by the shoulder of his coat. The Sten gun clattered briefly. Two of the archers slumped to the snow like scythe-cut grain. The others, with a wail of terror, fled. (It was, it seemed, their first taste of fire-arms.) Everything was noise, confusion and pandemonium, as, in the glow of the burning hut, we freed the dogs, leaped on to the sledge, and shot across the square. We careered through the village, our Sten gun aclatter, tossing our sticks of dynamite right, left and center. No wonder we were more than the Eskimoes cared to face! The few who were brave (or foolish) enough to try to halt us were scattered by a few well-placed sticks of dynamite; and in less time than it takes to describe we were clear of the houses and tearing at a mad gallop straight for the causeway, and the stockade.

It wouldn't have surprised me if the girl had been too terrified to join us, but some fifty yards clear of the huts she came running out from behind an outcrop of rock. I slowed down. As we passed, she jumped on to the runners and Somerville hauled her aboard.

"Look!" Ross pointed to the stockade.

Across the gateway the Eskimoes were starting to lower a barrier; a cross between a gate and a boom.

"Quick!" I shouted. "Straight at 'em. Before they get it in place."

I whipped up the dogs. Headlong we dashed at the entrance. Our last two sticks of dynamite brought the barrier down with a crash. And with a sickening lurching bounce, we tore through the splintered gateway and out into the snow. Ahead, in a broad uninterrupted sweep, ran the causeway leading to the crest of the nearest plateau. Behind, the glare of torches and reeds faded gradually into the mist; the shouting and the howling of dogs weakened and died. And we were free.

Ross wiped the sweat from his forehead.

"Never thought we'd make it!" he panted.

"We're not," I reminded him, "out of the wood yet. We may be followed. And we've only five dogs."

For some time—I should say about a quarter of an hour—we sledged on in silence, picking our way carefully through the clinging layers of mist which lay in the hollows like clouds of white cotton wool. It was still dark. The terrain was difficult. And progress was slow.

"Listen!"

Somerville raised his hand.

Faintly above the hiss of our runners we heard, far behind us, the long-drawn howl of huskies hitting the trail.

"Can't we go faster?" Ross's voice was anxious.

"In this mist!" I grunted. "We'd pile up."

Then an idea came to me.

"Freyja"—I spoke to the girl in Eskimo—"could you drive?"

She nodded.

"Could you drive faster than me?"

She nodded again. And I handed her the steering bar.

"For God's sake, man!" The captain looked at me as though I had gone off my head.

"If you've a better idea," I snapped, "let's have it. Otherwise shut up!"

She drove far faster than I would have dared. For one thing she knew the way. For another—as I afterwards discovered—her tribe had lived for so long in the mist that they had the knack of being able automatically to focus their eyes that ten degrees off-center which gives the longest vision in bad visibility (a technique cultivated, according to Ross, by night-fighter pilots during the war). Soon we were tearing through the darkness at a mad, nerve-tingling gallop. Outcrops of rock flashed by on either side. Once we tore through a warm-water spring. The sledge skidded and slithered and swayed; several times it nearly capsized. But fast as we went, our pursuers continued to gain: slowly but surely, Somerville picked up one of the Sten guns.

"Not much ammunition," he said.

"How much?"

"A hundred rounds. Maybe a hundred and twenty."

"Don't use it," I said, "unless you have to."

I spoke to Freyja. She cottoned on pretty quickly to

what was wanted, and her reply was just what I had hoped for.

"Listen," I said to the others, "she knows a place we can hide. Seems there's a river ahead: a big one. If we float down it, they'll have no trail to follow. Then we can lie up. Among the reeds."

"Won't it be frozen?" Ross was skeptical.

But when I translated the question the girl's reply was reassuring.

"She says it's ice-free," I told him. "Fed by hot springs."

"It's a chance." Somerville's voice was decisive. "Let's take it."

A few minutes later we swung aside into a narrow ravine, the incline of which grew gradually steeper. Ahead, the mist suddenly thickened. And there, right at our feet, was the river.

"Grab the guns," I shouted.

A splash like the belly-flop of a hippo, and we were up to our necks in a tepid, strongly flowing flood. We hadn't time to secure the lashings on the sledge. We'd barely time to grab the guns and skis, and hang for dear life on to the steering bar, before we were floating downstream in the grip of a steady five-knot current. In the blanket of mist which lay thickly over the water, I could hear the others threshing about, coughing and choking, but I could see nothing.

"You all right?" I called out anxiously.

"I am"—this was Somerville—"but I've lost one of the skis."

"Ross?"

He was almost alongside me; spluttering, and spitting water, and hanging on to the steering bar with one hand and the guns with the other. He seemed to be in pain.

"You O.K.?"

He nodded, but I noticed he kept his left arm pressed close to his side.

Freyja, I could hear splashing about alongside the dogs, guiding them to where the current flowed most strongly; she, it was obvious, was well able to look after herself. For some minutes we drifted along in silence; flotsam in the grip of the flood. It was a queer sensation, but one that was not—once we had got used to it—at all unpleasant. For the water was warm, the sledge floated

119

well, and we simply hung on to the back of it—like barnacles attached to a drifting hulk.

"This is a crazy idea," Ross grunted. "We'll all be drowned!"

"Better drowned," I said, "than stuck full of arrows."

We drifted on, the mist pulsating thickly round us like steam out of a saucepan. Suddenly, from far upstream, came a muffled splash. We looked at each other uneasily. The men with yellow hair, it seemed, were still on our trail.

"If they've more dogs than we have," Somerville said suddenly, "they'll be heavier. They'll drift faster."

The same thought evidently occurred to Freyja, for a second later she turned Queequeg's head for the shore.

"We must hide now." Her voice came out of the mist. "We must make no noise."

We edged towards the farther bank. The current was more sluggish here. And colder, far colder. Something brushed against my legs, and I jerked them away in fright; but it was only reeds, a cluster of coarse bulrushy reeds. Soon we could see ahead of us more patches of reeds; the outposts of a mighty host which now loomed out of the mist like Lilliputian *tirailleurs*. We nosed into the middle of them, following a narrow lane of open water. At first the going was easy; but soon the lane became increasingly shallow, muddy and cold. The reeds thickened until they hemmed us completely in. And eventually the lane degenerated into an ice-layered quagmire of mud, through which we had to haul the reluctant sledge and even more reluctant dogs. At last we floundered into the center of a veritable thicket, over which the mist hung especially thick—like an evil voluminous shroud. Here, with the mud up to our thighs, we came to a halt, panting, sodden and trembling with cold. At least Ross, Somerville and I were panting and trembling; Freyja, I noticed, seemed to take this sort of thing in her stride! She sat on the edge of the sledge, wringing the water out of her long golden hair, and breathing hardly more quickly than usual. What with the mist and the reeds, visibility was no more than a couple of yards; and it seemed to me that as long as we kept quiet there was precious little chance of our being found —for the mud had oozed back to cover our trail. But could we keep quiet? The dogs, of course, were the prob-

lem. They hated the mud—and no wonder, for they kept
sinking in up to their shoulders, whining, struggling clear,
scrabbling among the reeds for a foothold, only once
again to start sinking in. We decided to haul them on to
the sledge. Now a full-grown husky—dry—weighs something over fifty pounds. Ours were sodden and caked with
mud, and I reckon they weighed all of eighty pounds
apiece; we couldn't get a decent foothold; Ross had
strained his left arm while hanging on to our gun; and if it
hadn't been for Freyja I doubt if we would have managed
it. She was slightly built and almost fragile-looking; but
she was certainly strong—and after thirty years' whaling
in the Arctic I am a fair judge of strength. Between us we
managed to hoist the huskies on to the sledge; and then at
last they were quiet.

We were not a moment too soon. We had barely got the
last dog settled, when I heard Somerville catch his breath.
I looked up. And there, moving slowly towards us above
the reeds, was a luminous ball of fire: a halo of golden
light, moving apparently of its own volition. A second of
shocked surprise, then I realized what it was: a torch: a
resinous torch: its light refracted and magnified by the
mist until it resembled a miniature sun. I knew, too, who
was carrying the torch: one of the men with yellow hair.

We froze. I don't know how the others felt, but I for
one was terrified. My throat went dry, and my heart began
to pound away like a sledge-hammer. For our guns were
coated in mud and ice; they might well be blocked; and
even if they weren't, the first shot would certainly bring
the whole tribe swarming about our ears.

The light came on, heading directly towards us.

Desperately we looked about for a way of escape. But
escape there was none. For on either side of us other
torches, faint and diffused, were yellowing the mist, and it
was all too clear what was happening: the Eskimoes were
combing the marsh, were working their way through the
reeds in an extended line. And we—as ill-luck would have
it—were in the direct line of advance of one of their
search-parties.

Somerville reached for the Sten gun, Ross and I for our
rifles.

"Don't fire," I hissed, "till you're certain he's seen us."

The torch came nearer. We heard footsteps, the sucking

121

sound of splatchers pulling away from mud, and out of the corner of my eye I noticed Freyja crawling away among the reeds to our left. I couldn't blame her, and yet —quite illogically—I felt a stab of disappointment (I had hoped, I suppose, that she would see things through with us). The light came steadily on: huge, luminous, mesmerizing. It was almost on top of us now. Then suddenly, from among the reeds to our left, came a splash, followed a second later by the click-click-click of a marsh bird. Or was it a marsh bird? The light came to a stop. We could see the torch moving uncertainly to and fro; it was so close to us that individual flames were clearly visible. Then —again from the reeds to our left—another splash, another click-click-click. And the torch moved away at right angles towards the noise. Somerville and I looked at each other. We could see the light rising and falling, as, less than a dozen feet from where we were crouched, the man with yellow hair peered and prodded among the reeds, where only a few seconds before Freyja had disappeared. Any second, I thought, and he'll find her. It's inevitable: as certain as night follows day. But I was wrong. He searched carefully and for a long time, while the other torches, on either side of us, moved steadily on. Then he gave up. We heard him mutter angrily as he went splashing away, moving fast to catch up with the others. He passed about nine feet from the sledge, but he didn't see us, and soon he had vanished into the mist.

"He must have walked slap over the top of her!" I whispered.

"Come on." Somerville started to push through the reeds.

We searched everywhere, but we found nothing. It was quite incredible. The girl had completely vanished.

Soon the torches were out of sight, the men with yellow hair out of earshot.

"Freyja," I whispered softly, "Where are you?"

Silence. And all around us the mist seething and writhing like a pit of snakes. I shivered—and only partly with cold.

"Freyja!" My voice sounded hollow and frightened. "They've gone. It's safe now."

Almost under my feet the mud stirred. Beside me a group of reeds swayed as though in the wind—but there was no wind. Then, to my amazement, I saw breath, human breath, spiraling out of the reed stems. And a second later we were digging her out of the mud.

She had been lying, totally submerged, at the bottom of a pool of ice-coated water, breathing through the hollow stems of the reeds. To say she was covered in mud would be an understatement. It seemed as if she *was* mud: solid, oozing mud from head to foot. And the mud was ice-cold. By the time we got her out she was frozen almost literally solid; was too cold by far to either speak or move. We laid her out on the sledge, stripped off her mud-soaked clothes, covered her up with all the blankets we had, and started to try and massage her back to life. It was a near thing—another five minutes and I reckon she could well have died of exposure. As it was, under the combined effect of blankets and pummeling, she at last lost her frightening rigidity; her skin began to flush pink under its blueness; her eyes opened and her teeth started to chatter. We knew then that she was going to pull through. For the second time in less than a dozen hours she had saved our lives.

We huddled together beside the sledge, up to our thighs in mud, shivering with fright and cold. Although for the moment we were safe, it would have been hard to picture a more bedraggled and miserable quartet.

"We can't stay here," I muttered to Somerville. "We'll freeze to death."

He nodded. "We'd best pull for the shore."

We sorted out the traces, tied the leads round our waists, and moved slowly off. I tried to persuade Freyja to stay on the sledge; but she wouldn't have it; she insisted on hauling away with the rest of us. It went against the grain to see her, after all she had gone through, floundering about in the mud. But I dare say she knew best; for sledge-hauling was certainly good for the circulation! Anyhow, I kept a careful eye on her, and noticed that after a while she began to move less stiffly, to pull more strongly, and eventually her teeth stopped chattering.

It took us a full half-hour to force a way ashore: half an hour of hard back-breaking work, with the dogs useless in the mud, and our having, for the greater part of the way, to haul them as well as the sledge. However, as we neared the bank the going got easier; and at last—thankfully—we clambered up on to firm ground.

The mist was still thick but the light was less sepulchral now, and I judged it was past dawn—though with Somerville's watch broken in our dive into the river, this was something we could only guess at. There wasn't a sign of the men with yellow hair; but we were taking no chances; we moved quietly and spoke only in whispers.

Our first need was obviously to find somewhere to lie up: a place where we could light a fire, get ourselves warm and dry, and have some sleep. I gathered from Freyja that a couple of miles back from the river was a rocky plateau, the base of which was honeycombed with caves. It sounded a likely place—provided the Eskimoes hadn't guessed our intentions and got there first—and we agreed to head for it.

And for once things worked out according to plan. After less than an hour's sledging we came to the caves: a series of dark labyrinthine clefts hollowed out of a fault in the volcanic rock by water during the summer thaw. We scrambled past the larger, more obvious openings and chose a small, well-hidden cave that was sheltered and could be easily defended. We soon got a fire going, well back from the entrance, and before long we had dried out both ourselves and our guns. As soon as we were warm and dry, we ate; and as soon as we had eaten we slept, turn and turn about.

Ross and Somerville dossed down first, an arrangement which suited me well; for while they slept I could talk to Freyja. And there was plenty I wanted to ask her.

We built up the fire, then sat down together at the mouth of the cave, looking out over the mist-filled valley.

We were an incongruous pair. I doubt if many of my fellow whalers would have recognized their erstwhile Fangst Leader now—for in the last few weeks I must have lost over a stone in weight, and my hair and beard hadn't been cut for months. While I am willing to bet that Freyja's own family would have been hard put to recognize her—for she was wearing the trousers of a professor of McGill University, the monkey-jacket of a retired naval officer, and a Hudson's Bay Company blanket draped like a shawl over her head! For a while we sat side by side in silence, keeping anxious lookout for the tell-tale blobs of light which would warn us that the Eskimoes were again on our trail. What she was thinking of I had no means of telling; but her thoughts, it seemed to me, could hardly be happy. Even assuming that she and Ross's son were lovers and she thought she was going to find him, she had left so many familiar things—home and family and tribe—for the sake of a very outside chance of happiness. I looked at her. She might well, I thought, find it a relief to talk; I certainly would be glad to listen.

"Freyja," I said, "will you tell me about your people?"

11

The Last of the Vikings

"ARE my people so strange," she said, "that you want to know our history?"

"Not strange," I lied, as I thought diplomatically, "just unexpected. Take your hair, for example. Most people who live in the Arctic have dark hair; yet yours is fair, and," I added, "very beautiful."

Her eyes became suddenly watchful.

"I am not a child," she said coldly, "to be flattered with pretty words. What do you want to know?"

I had been put—very properly—in my place; and yet I wasn't angry; indeed if anything my opinion of Freyja went up. She was obviously a young lady to be reckoned with.

"I'm sorry." I looked at her curiously. "Will you forget what I said? And tell me about your people?"

I thought at first that she was going to refuse; for several minutes she said nothing, gave no indication of having even heard what I said. Then, simply:

"Where do you want me to start?"

"Start at the beginning: as far back as your history goes."

She looked out across the mist-filled valley. "Many generations ago," she said, "My people lived in another country, far away towards the rising sun. The land they lived in was barren—or so the Shamen tell us—with much ice and little food, and the people suffered much from hunger. Sometimes ships would come, bringing food; but as the generations passed the ships came less often, and the people grew even hungrier. At last, becoming desperate, they decided to leave the barren land. They built ships; and some sailed towards the setting sun, and some towards the rising. Only those too weak to travel were left behind; and these soon died." [1]

"And your people," I prompted, "they sailed towards the setting sun?"

She nodded.

"There were five ships, the Shamen say, each carrying about fifty people: men, women and children. Day after day they sailed towards the sunset, until at last, after a voyage of many perils, they sighted a strange new land with forests sweeping down to the sea. Here they landed. They built a village close to the shore, and for a time they prospered. But one night the men who lived in the forests dressed themselves up as birds, with painted feathers fixed in their hair. They gained entry to the village by treachery, and burnt it, killing many. The few who survived—less than a hundred of us—fled to the boats and pushed out to sea. Next morning as soon as it was light they returned to the shore, and there in front of their village they saw those who had been captured—their own mothers, husbands and daughters—being burnt alive by the birdmen. Our men would have rushed ashore and fought till they died; but Loki, the priest, persuaded them not to. That way, he said they would only be killed; they would gain nothing; there would be no revenge; he, he said, had a better way. And that night, as the last boat-load of our people headed north, he made them swear a great oath—that until the day of Ragnarok [2] they would wage war against the bird-men; that they would neither live with them, nor trade

[1] A friend of Professor Somerville, who is a Lecturer in History at McGill, tells me that the above is a pretty succinct description of the Viking colonization of Greenland. And—as further evidence of the origin of Freyja's tribe—their language is very akin to that of the Greenland Eskimo. K. R.

[2] The day, according to Norse folk-lore, when the world will perish in the last great conflict between giants and gods. K. R.

with them, nor have any sort of dealings with them. And so," Freyja sighed, "it has always been; and so it always will be, for as many generations as there are fawns in a herd of caribou. Our people never break an oath."

"And the last boat-load?" I queried. "They found their way here?"

"Not for many years," she said. "Little is known about what happened next; but it seems that for several generations there was much fighting and much moving from place to place, with our people being driven even farther north into the land of ice and snow. For a time it is thought they followed the caribou herds, from sea to sea; then, it seems, they lived on the shore of a great bay, hunting whales. And it was here, the Shamen say, that our people first heard of the Lost Ones."

"Go on," I said.

"It seems that on the shore of the bay there were Eskimoes, who also lived by hunting whales. In time our people got to hear of their legend; the legend that when the whales are dying they go to a great graveyard at the mouth of hell. Now the Eskimoes were frightened of the graveyard. They dared not go near it. But our people were not frightened—not then. And they knew that if only they could find the graveyard, the dead whales would provide them with food. So they set out to search for it. For many generations they searched in vain, wandering farther and farther north. They suffered much from cold and blizzard and hunger. Many died. And at last only eighteen were left. Then, when hope was almost exhausted, these eighteen came to the land of the mist, where water rises warm from the earth. And here they found the graveyard."

She paused.

"And in the graveyard," I prompted, "they found the magic stones, inside the Lost Ones?"

Her eyes became suddenly troubled.

"Not," she said slowly, "to start with. At first, I think, our people lived alongside the graveyard; and all who were brave enough to pass the mouth of hell could go there; and meat and skin and oil and bone were theirs for the taking. But when Loki found the stone things were different."

"In what way?" I was puzzled.

She seemed uncertain how to explain. Then—unexpectedly—she launched into a long, muddled paean of praise of Loki and the Shamen: how they had discovered the magic stone that gave promise of life everlasting; how they alone were worthy of touching the stone; how they alone were good enough to pass the mouth of hell without being punished by the gods; how they alone were brave enough to take the stone from out of the jaws of the guardians. It was only slowly, by dint of much questioning, that I was able to piece together what had really happened.

It was, I suppose, a story as old as civilization itself: a story, according to Somerville, which has its parallel in the rise of the priest cults in a dozen or more countries—Crete, Tibet and Egypt; Greece, Judea and Peru. What happens in every case is this. The Shamen (or priests), being the most intelligent of the race, make a certain discovery; they then use this discovery as the basis of a religious cult, with themselves as the privileged acolytes. In the case of Freyja's people it was easy for an outsider such as myself to put two and two together and see what had happened. As I understood it, one of the Shamen must have discovered how to make scent out of ambergris, how to turn the fatty lumps of mucus found in the stomachs of certain whales into *"the MoSt bewitchen Sent of Flowers."* Now the Shamen's first step, I gathered, was simply to see that the process of manufacture was kept secret, remained a monopoly of the priests. For several generations, it seems, they were content to be the sole purveyors of a commodity which was—at least among the women—in great demand. From here it was an easy and obvious step for them to increase the value of the scent by investing it with some sort of religious significance. Now the way they did this struck me as being very clever. The religion of Freyja's people, as far as I could make out, was a curious mixture of Christianity (inherited from their Norse ancestors in Greenland) and Eskimo taboos (picked up during their migrations); and the Shamen managed, very cunningly, to bring the tenets of the two together in a way that suited them down to the ground. They started the custom of giving each child, at birth, a locket filled with scent. This locket (as long as it remained full of scent) was supposed to act, in life, as a talisman: a keeper-away of ill fortune. And in death (again as long as it was full of scent) it was supposed to act as a sort of passport to heaven: a key to the life hereafter. Imagine the value this gave to the scent! Imagine the power it gave to those who had the monopoly of the scent's manufacture! Soon only one thing was needed to establish the Shamen in absolute authority. They had to make certain that nobody else stumbled across the secret of how to make scent out of ambergris: they had, in other words, to establish a monopoly in handling the dead whales.

Now a way to do this was ready made. The only means of access to the graveyard was, I gathered, *via* the mouth of hell: a difficult and dangerous route. Far too difficult and far too dangerous, the Shamen began to suggest, for ordinary men and women. For the gods would become angry if every Tom, Dick and Harry looked down through the mouth of hell and saw the secrets of what went on in the bowels of the earth: such mysteries were things that only Shamen should know. And eventually, I gathered from Freyja, after much talk and a full-scale civil war, the priests won their point, and the tribe moved away from the graveyard and settled on the shore of the lake where their village stands today. From then on no one but the Shamen was allowed to visit the graveyard. Which meant that, quite apart from controlling the manufacture of scent, the priests also gained control over the tribe's principal source of food, oil, leather and the hundred-and-one by-products of the dead whales. No wonder their power soon became absolute! And no wonder, too, that they guarded the secret of the graveyard with such sedulous zeal, carefully cultivating the myth that Prince Patrick Island was forbidden ground, invoking the oath of Ragnarok to keep the fair-haired people a tribe apart and to frighten off or kill all outsiders who set foot in their highly profitable domain.

I could see now how it all fitted in: the fear of the neighboring Eskimoes, the fact that the whereabouts of the graveyard had remained a secret all these hundreds of years, and the fact that the men with yellow hair had remained a race apart—untainted by intermarriage—the last of the Vikings.

I ought, I think, to make it clear that while, according to my way of thinking, the Shamen were complete and utter charlatans—purveyors of a hotchpotch of convenient taboos—Freyja saw them in quite a different light. To her

130

they were demigods, beyond reproach or criticism, father confessors *par excellence*. I did try suggesting that things had worked out uncommonly well for them. But she wouldn't have it. I would have stood more chance of convincing a Roman Catholic that his priest was heretical. And it was while we were arguing on this point that I realized, very clearly, something which I had been in danger these last few hours of forgetting: the fact that Freyja, for all her dignity and courage, for all her beauty and obvious refinement, was at heart a native: a superstitious savage whose life was governed by tribal lore and pagan rituals utterly beyond our comprehension.

Her world and our world, it seemed to me, were too far apart to be bridged. And in that—if ever we did manage to find young Ross—I could see the seeds of tragedy.

12

In Such Stillness the World Was Born

THAT night each of us managed to get eight hours of good uninterrupted sleep; and next morning, strengthened and refreshed, we prepared to set out for the graveyard.

On Freyja's advice we decided not to use any of the normal and comparatively easy routes along the valley, but to make our way via a little known path directly over the plateaus and so drop down to the graveyard from an unexpected direction. Our object in this, of course, was to avoid making contact with the men with yellow hair, who by this time were pretty certain to have guessed our destination and to have sealed off all the obvious approaches. Somerville suggested hopefully that if we lay low for a while perhaps they would give the search up; but Freyja shook her head.

"As long as you search for the magic stone," she said, "they will search for you."

It was an uncomfortable thought.

It was, according to the girl, roughly twenty miles to the graveyard, and she added, as early that morning we were preparing to set out, that the journey would take us "about a week." It sounded a long time to cover so short a distance; but in the end her estimate proved over-optimistic.

For the terrain turned out to be unbelievably difficult.

Our first task was to climb the plateau immediately behind us. It wasn't very high—no more than some hundred and fifty feet in fact—but its walls were smooth and sheer: unclimbable it seemed to me for men, let alone for dogs. But Freyja pointed out an unstable-looking chimney: a near-vertical crack in the rock.

"That is the way," she said.

At Somerville's suggestion we unhitched the dogs, and prepared to use their harness as rope. Freyja, however, didn't go much on the idea of being roped, and she started up the chimney alone. She made steady progress, and after scrambling like a cat over a hair-raising overhang, reached a small ledge about half-way up. From here she watched our laborious preparations.

"Throw me your rope," she called down gaily, "and I will haul you in. Like three harpooned whales!"

"Damned if I'm going to be hauled up by a girl!" grunted Ross.

And after much panting, scrambling, slithering and sweating, he and I managed to claw our way up. We then paid out the harness to Somerville, who secured the huskies to the end of it for us to haul up, one at a time. It took us five hours to get ourselves, our sledge, dogs and stores on to the half-way ledge. Freyja wanted to go on; but by this time Ross and I were utterly exhausted, and we agreed to pitch camp on the ledge. It was not a comfortable site but at least it was sheltered, and we slept well.

Next day it took us another three hours to struggle as far as the top of the plateau. We had hoped that from here on the going might be easier; but as we emerged over the rim and saw what lay ahead our hearts sank.

It was a fantastic scene we looked down on. Ahead of us the plateau sloped gently away from its circumference to form a vast natural amphitheater perhaps five or six hundred acres in extent. And—to our amazement—the whole of the floor of the amphitheater was strewn with craters, ash-cones and fantastic outcrops of volcanic excrescence. In a world of lunar-like confusion, I counted eleven ash-cones, rising like slag-heaps out of a gigantic coalfield, five extinct craters, sunk like static whirlpools into a sea of rock; and in the very center two dark chaotic pyramids, some hundred feet in height, pulsating steam—apparently the sole living organisms in a world that was otherwise dormant, its creative impulse spent. There seemed no way across it that wasn't fraught with the most appalling difficulty and danger.

"Can't we work round the edge?" Somerville suggested.

But Freyja shook her head, pointing to where, on either side of us, the rim dropped sharply into the amphitheater in cliffs which were low but completely sheer: unclimbable even to a team of Alpine guides. There was no alternative. So down into the amphitheater we went.

At first our route lay over a number of not too difficult snow-cornices; but as we worked lower these gave way to virgin rock. And what rock it was! Yellow and ochre and purplish-red, the different strata lay in higgledy-piggledy terraces, still crinkled with the heat in which they had been prised out of the innards of the earth. Across them ran fissures, some only a few inches deep, others—black as polished shale—dropping sheer to unfathomable depths. And, as we worked our way forward, we discovered that the central pyramids were not, after all, the only active parts of the amphitheater; for out of the deeper fissures rose spirals of steam; hot, wispy vapor; the very breath of creation. It was a terrifying world we descended into; all the more terrifying for its complete and utter silence. For, as we watched the steam pulsating out of the ground in silent frenzy, we all of us had the feeling that only a little way beneath the surface titanic forces were straining at the leash, were held in check under a tension all the more wicked for the unnatural graveyard quiet. In such stillness, I thought, the world was born. And maybe its birth pangs were not yet over.

Slowly, testing every foothold, we edged our way forward. We could only hope that Freyja knew where she was leading us.

There must, I suppose, have been a path of sorts: a trail she could somehow recognize and follow. I only know that we seemed to wander, hour after hour, in and out of the terraces of rock, skirting the fissures, the fumaroles and the occasional steaming lakes. It was a nightmare journey.

One particularly hellish place I shall never forget. For about fifty yards we had to scramble along a narrow ledge which slanted across the side of a cliff. Beneath the ledge, the rocks had been badly eroded, scalloped into a fresco of wheel-like cogs; and lapping the base of these, some twenty feet below us, was a lake of boiling mud: a lake that steamed and plopped obscenely like a saucepan of overheated gruel. A slip was something that didn't bear thinking of.

"You would like to camp here for the night?" Freyja's voice was solemn.

"Don't be damned silly," I grunted.

"I thought perhaps you liked to camp on ledges?"

She was in high spirits that day, and for all the early part of the journey. But after a while even her energy began to flag, even her vitality became sucked dry. And no wonder. For it took us five days to cross the amphitheater: five days of clawing our way with painful slowness through labyrinths of volcanic rock: five days of choking and coughing in the hot sulphur-laden air: five days of picking a path through a welter of chasms, fumaroles and mud lakes—where a single slip would have led to the most appalling death.

But everything, for those who endure long enough, comes to an end; and at last, late on the afternoon of the sixth day, we approached the amphitheater's farther rim. Soon we could see ahead of us the snow-cornices which comprised our last step out of the devil's cauldron. And how we longed to plunge into them! For after nearly a week among the volcanic terraces we were dusty and parched and impregnated with sulphur. It was amazing how the fine yellow particles had worked themselves into every fiber of our clothing and every pore of our bodies, until I at any rate felt as though my skin had taken on a permanent yellow pigmentation, like the skin of a dried and crinkled apricot!

In the event, the cornices didn't entirely come up to expectation—for even the snow was dirty with sulphur. But at least it was cool. And that evening, as for the first time in over a week we drank and sponged ourselves down in ice-cold water, our spirits began to revive. Our morale had a further boost when Freyja announced that the graveyard was only five or six miles beyond the rim of the amphitheater, and that we would, with luck, get there the following afternoon. It seemed almost too good to be true.

We could hardly believe that at long last, after all our vicissitudes, our goal was practically in sight.

Next morning we scaled the cornices in less than a couple of hours, scrambled eagerly out of the amphitheater, and stood looking down on the coastline beyond. The view was partly encouraging, partly anticlimax. Encouraging because ahead of us the snow-covered hills sloped down in easy gradients to the sea; so the going for the last stage to the graveyard promised to be reasonably good. Anticlimax because the coast itself was shrouded in mist: thick, impenetrable mist, rising up from the sea and blanketing the line of the shore like a well-laid smoke-screen. Right up to the last second, it seemed, the secret of the graveyard was being jealously guarded.

"Which way?" I turnd to Freyja.

She didn't answer at first, but when I repeated the question she pointed away to the left, to where a broad, well-defined valley ran down to the sea. And I noticed that, as she pointed, she averted her eyes. I remembered something then that I hadn't thought of for days: that the graveyard was strictly taboo, and that to get to it we would have to pass through the mouth of hell. I hoped that Freyja wasn't going to have last-minute qualms about showing us the way.

"Come on," I said, "if we want to get there before dark."

And we started off down the valley at a spanking gallop.

At first we made excellent progress. But as we neared the sea the mist became increasingly thick, and Freyja increasingly nervous. After a while she began to lag behind. I could guess how she felt. When she had first agreed to bring us to the graveyard, the hope of finding Donald had more than counterbalanced her fear of breaking the taboo. While crossing the amphitheater, physical hardship and moment-to-moment dangers had precluded her looking ahead. But now that we were actually approaching our goal, her fears had come back. Overwhelmingly. It was not surprising, really. After all, her life up to now had been wholly conditioned by tribal lore; and the prospect of breaking a taboo (especially one of such significance as was laid on the graveyard) must have held terrors for her that were too deeply rooted for us to even start to understand. After a while she stopped altogether.

"You go on," she said. "I will stay here."

We halted, uncertainly.

"I think," I said, "we ought to keep together."

Her eyes flashed in sudden anger.

"Don't be afraid," she said, "I'm not going to run away."

"Tell her," Somerville cut in quickly, "that we don't want to leave her alone. In case we're being watched."

It looked like an impasse; but at last, after much persuasion, we managed to get her on the move again—though only on the understanding that when we neared the edge of the cliffs we would leave her and go on for the last few yards by ourselves to look down into the graveyard.

And that is how it worked out. As soon as we neared the shore we halted close to a little outcrop of rock; and Freyja pointed to the cliff-edge, some fifty yards ahead.

"You can see the Lost Ones," she whispered, "from there."

"Come on!" Ross was impatient.

For a second Somerville and I hung back. Then in an eager rush we were scrambling towards the edge of the cliff.

13

The Mouth of Hell

AT the edge of the cliff the rocks were slippery, veneered in ice. We edged forward cautiously, expectantly. And there, far below us, lay the graveyard of the whales: fantastic as an opium smoker's pipe-dream, macabre as a woodcut of Dante's *Inferno*.

For several minutes we clung to the ice-coated rocks in silence, too amazed to speak. For this is what we saw.

Some five hundred feet below us lay a large horseshoe bay, ice-free and ringed by towering black cliffs, sheer as the masts of a tea-clipper. At the foot of the cliffs was a strip of beach: a narrow riband of coarse grey sand. And strewn close-packed along the beach lay the carcasses of whales: whales by the thousand: Grey, Bottle-nosed and Beluga; Bowhead, White-beaked and Sperm. They lay in heaped-up confusion; like corpses after a battle; like so many logs of driftwood tossed up in the wake of a storm.

"Eureka!" Somerville's voice was awestruck.

Ross shaded his eyes against the glare of the westering sun. "My son will be there," he whispered. "I know it."

I said nothing. I was too busy studying the carcasses. Even from the top of the cliff I could tell that almost half of them were Sperm—I could recognize their great lopsided heads, a third the length of their bodies.

138

"Must be ambergris there by the ton!" I whispered. "But how do we get down?"

We studied the cliffs carefully, section by section, searching for some sort of break. But none was visible.

"If the Eskimoes get down," Ross grunted, "so can we."

"They," I reminded him, "get down via the mouth of hell. Wherever that is."

"Could be there." Somerville pointed to the opposite side of the bay.

It was hard in the evening light to be sure of details—especially as the part of the bay to which he pointed was in shadow—but following the line of Somerville's finger I could just make out a dark circular opening, where, it seemed to me, a river came flowing out through a subterranean tunnel at the base of the cliff. We strained our eyes; and at last I managed to make out what was happening. There *was* an opening at the bottom of the cliff, and it *was* the mouth of an underground river: only the river was tidal, and, at the present moment, the water was flowing not out of its mouth but into it. Then, as I was about to turn away, I noticed something else; something which made me a hundred per cent certain that we must indeed be looking at the mouth of the Eskimo hell. For I saw, rolling over and over in the fast-flowing tide rip, the carcass of a whale—a great sixty-foot Sperm—being borne in through the mouth of the river; and I remembered the Eskimo legend; that the whales came to the graveyard to die, and that, as soon as they are dead, their bodies are tipped down through the mouth of hell into the waters under the earth.

But it was one thing to know where the mouth of hell was, and another to get down to it.

"There must be *some* way down!" Ross was impatient. "Let's ask the girl."

I felt suddenly guilty. I had forgotten her. I turned round quickly, anxiously, half afraid she might have vanished. But she was still there, sitting on the outcrop of rock exactly where we had left her. As we made our way back, I noticed that she was twisting and untwisting the cord of her locket. She seemed hardly to notice our return.

"Freyja," I said, "how do we get down to the graveyard?"

She didn't answer. She went on twisting her locket.

Ross snapped his fingers impatiently. "Tell her to pull herself together," he muttered.

Somerville turned on him. "Leave her alone," he snapped. "Can't you see she's scared stiff?"

We stood in an awkward circle, a little way back from the edge of the cliffs, an evening breeze swirling occasional eddies of mist about our knees. In the sudden silence I became aware of a strange sound: a muffled boom-boom-boom from somewhere way under our feet: like the muted throb of subterranean drums: or was it a subterranean river?

"It's too late," I said, "to try and get down tonight. Let's camp."

We decided, out of deference to Freyja, to move away from the cliffs—for the prospect of even looking into the graveyard seemed to appall her. We therefore hauled round the dogs and headed inland towards an area of volcanic rock a little way up the valley.

It was almost dark when we stumbled across the igloo.

Somerville saw it first: the heap of half-collapsed snow-blocks silhouetted like a bomb-blasted building in the path of the setting sun. It looked derelict and long-deserted; one side and most of the roof had collapsed into the surrounding snow. We pulled the dogs to a halt. For several seconds we stared at the igloo in silence. Then Ross said quietly, "I'm going to look inside."

I grabbed hold of him. "Let me look."

But he shook himself free and ran quickly towards the igloo. The same fear had caught at us both: if the igloo was Donald's—and who else's *could* it be—mightn't his body by lying inside? We left the dogs. We rushed towards the igloo. We peered in through the shattered walls. We clawed away at the fallen snow. We dug deep and for a long time. But we found nothing.

"Thank God," Ross whispered. "He's not here."

I turned to Freyja. "Would any of your people build an igloo like this?" I asked her.

She examined the crude, ill-graded snow-blocks, and shook her head.

Two things seemed obvious. The igloo was Donald's. And it was some time since he had used it.

"But it *is* proof he got to the graveyard." Ross's eyes were shining. "Let's give him a signal. Maybe he'll hear it. Maybe he'll answer."

"Don't bank too much," I said, "on his being able to answer."

But Ross wouldn't be put off. "Let's fire the guns!" His eagerness was almost pitiable.

Well, I didn't go much on the idea; for if the Eskimoes were still searching for us it would give away our position. But on the other hand, I could appreciate how Ross must be feeling. The truth was so near; it was hard to postpone the final grasping of it. "All right," I said slowly. "But one salvo, and one salvo only."

The reports rang out, sharp and startlingly loud in the quiet Arctic twilight. We waited, keyed-up, for a reply. But—not surprisingly—none came. Ross skied across to the edge of the cliffs and peered down into the gathering darkness; but he saw no movement, no sign of life. It wasn't to be wondered at. It would have been surprising if we *had* had a reply. But all the same, we were left with a feeling of acute disappointment.

We were unusually quiet that night as we pitched camp. All of us were keyed up: eager to get down to the graveyard, impatient at being balked—if only temporarily—with our goal actually in sight. And, to add to our troubles, Freyja was jumpy. It was clear that she was scared stiff of everything to do with the graveyard. Her nerves were strung taut: at every unexpected movement or sound she started and trembled; she was a different person to the girl who, only a week ago, had helped us escape from the Eskimo village. After supper I did my best to comfort her.

"What are you afraid of, Freyja?" I asked her.

For a long time she was silent; then she whispered, with a sort of helpless fatality. "Those who look into the mouth of hell die. The Shamen say so."

"And we have to go past the mouth of hell to get to the graveyard? Is that it?"

She said nothing. Her fingers plucked at her locket. Then to my intense embarrassment—she started to cry. She sat there perfectly motionless, not uttering a sound, the tears streaming down her face.

141

"Listen, Freyja." I took her hand. "Nobody can *make* you go past the mouth of hell. We'll find another way down."

But the tears didn't stop.

"There isn't another way." She wasn't wallowing in self-pity; she was simply stating a fact.

"Then I tell you what. We'll go farther along the coast. Get down to the sea where the cliffs are lower. Build a boat. And come into the graveyard by sea."

It struck me as being a harmless enough proposal. But Freyja's eyes widened in sudden terror. "No!" she gasped. "No!"

"All right, then," I said quickly. "You needn't come with us. Tell us the way and we'll go by ourselves."

But she shook her head. "I must come too."

I had a sudden flash of intuition. "I promise you," I said, "that if we find Donald in the graveyard, we'll bring him back to you."

Her tears stopped then. Her eyes became suddenly watchful. *"You* promise. But *he"*—she jerked her head to where Ross was patrolling outside the tent—*"he* will try to take Donald away from me."

I was appalled at her perceptiveness—for I had to admit she'd just about hit the nail on the head. I couldn't think what to say. Denials, excuses, explanations went racing through my mind; but they all seemed either dishonest or trivial. Then Freyja came to my rescue. She smiled: a small, unhappy smile. "Don't worry," she said simply. "Tomorrow I'll show you the way."

I felt relieved, yet at the same time acutely uncomfortable, acutely guilty. "That's fine, Freyja." I squeezed her hand—an expedient Judas squeeze. "And don't you," I added, "be scared. We'll look after you."

She said nothing. She just smiled. A small, unhappy smile.

We set out early the next morning, heading, to my surprise, not towards the shore, but inland, back up the valley. To begin with the terrain was easy and we made rapid progress; but after a couple of hours we began to traverse diagonally across the side of the valley, and here the going became increasingly difficult. For we were back in volcanic country now, and had to make frequent detours round craters and ridges of terraced lava.

It was while we were crossing a narrow ledge that I felt, quite out of the blue, a sudden stab of fear: an old, familiar fear. I pulled the dogs to a halt.

"What's up?" Ross came skiing across.

I looked carefully up and down valley.

"Maybe nothing. But I had the feeling our friends were back. Watching us."

We stood very still, scanning the valley methodically, section by section. Nothing moved.

"Imagination perhaps?" Somerville helped himself to snuff. "We're all pretty keyed up."

"Maybe. Maybe not." I turned to the girl. "How much farther to go, Freyja?"

She pointed to a volcanic-looking area less than a mile ahead.

"All right," I said. "We'll go on. But carefully. You two ski on ahead. See we don't run into an ambush."

Ross and Somerville made a good job of their scouting. They searched our line of advance and every inch of the volcanic area we were approaching. But they found nothing. And midday saw us halted on the rim of a large crater.

It was an eerie place: concentric circles of rock spiraling down like the swirls of a whirlpool: and at the bottom, the vortex: the gaping chasm of the fumarole, through which (when the volcano had been active) liquid lava had come flooding up, white-hot, from the innards of the earth. Freyja pointed to the fumarole.

"That is the way," she said.

Now just what lay ahead I couldn't imagine; but the fumarole was obviously no place for dogs. So we tethered them to an outcrop of rock, and began the descent by ourselves, carrying only our rucksacks and guns. I noticed that the snow in the crater was undisturbed. No ski tracks. No footprints. And, in consequence, no reception committee lying in wait for us. Soon we had slithered down to the mouth of the fumarole and were peering nervously into the dark and apparently bottomless chasm. It was about thirty feet in circumference, and tempered to the smoothness of a billiard ball. Freyja crawled round the rim of it, feeling for something below the surface. Then she lowered herself down.

"Follow me carefully." Her voice, strangely distorted, came echoing up from the depths. "Come down backwards. I will guide your feet."

I licked my lips. "Come on," I muttered. "If she can do it, so can we."

And we lowered ourselves cautiously into the mouth of the dead volcano.

For the first few steps we descended blind. I could feel Freyja's fingers guiding my feet into footholds—but whether these were natural footholds or ones which had been cut by man I couldn't tell. I, in turn, guided Ross's feet, and he in his guided Somerville's. It was a case, to start with, of the blind leading the blind. But as we descended, our eyes became gradually accustomed to the darkness, and after awhile we were able to make out what manner of place we were in. And, having seen, I for one would have preferred to stay in the dark!

For beneath us the fumarole opened out, rather like an inverted funnel. Its rock walls, hung with unstable sheets of ice, fell away steeply, and zigzagging down them I could make out the indeterminate outline of a path: a series of footholds cut into the rock and augmented here and there by iron pegs linked with guide ropes. To this frightening scene the lighting added a final touch of bizarreness. For through the mouth of the fumarole daylight came flooding in, white and unbelievably brilliant; so that from below the upper reaches of the funnel down which we descended looked as though they were bathed in harsh metallic light. The middle reaches, in contrast, were a patchwork of light and shade; light, where the hanging precipices of ice reflected the brightness from above; shade, where the rock walls hung bare; while the lower reaches, towards which we slowly descended, were filled with Stygian gloom. Filled, too, with a strange cacophony of sound: the boom and thresh of water racing through subterranean runnels somewhere way below our feet.

For a while we clawed our way down in silence, step by hesitating step. Then Ross started to whistle—I suppose in an effort to keep up his spirits.

"Stop that!" I hissed.

"Why?"

"You'll have the ice walls down."

We went on descending, hand over hand, in silence. I counted the footholds: one hundred, one hundred and fifty, two hundred; then the angle of descent began to ease off, and at last, panting and wet with sweat, we were standing on level ground: the floor of the fumarole, some two hundred feet under the ground.

It was an awe-inspiring place: rather like a vast windowless cathedral, with the ice walls looking like marble pillars supporting a roof so far above our heads it was out of sight. The air, to my surprise, was fresh and pleasantly warm; it was also atremble with noise: the continual boom and thresh of water. Straining our eyes we could just make out, on the farther side of the fumarole, the outline of a great subterranean river disappearing into the gloom. As soon as we had got back our breath I turned to Freyja.

"Which way now?" I asked her.

So far she had been surprisingly composed: a very model of sang-froid. But now, once again, she began to tremble.

"Which way now?" I asked her gently. "Tell me, and I'll go first."

She pointed towards the underground river.

I set out cautiously across the rocky floor of the fumarole. But she didn't follow. She sat down, breathing quickly.

"You go," she whispered. "I will stay here."

We huddled together at the bottom of the fumarole, listening to the boom-boom-boom of the river: an angry turmoil of sound, deep and menacing.

I looked at Freyja. "Does the noise come from the mouth of hell?"

She nodded, moistening her lips.

"Somerville," I said, "you stay with the girl. Don't move from where we are now, Ross, you and I'll have a look at the Nether Regions!"

We set out cautiously, groping our way towards the booming of the river. The light was poor, and as we moved away from the center of the fumarole it got worse rather than better. Soon we were stumbling forward in near-darkness. The booming and threshing grew louder, magnified in the enclosed funnel-like vault as sound-waves in an amplifier. Soon we could scarcely hear ourselves speak.

"Watch out!" I shouted to Ross. "Sounds pretty nasty ahead!"

A second later he pulled up short. And there at our very feet was the river: the great warm-water river (I guessed it was the one we had floated down, after our escape from the Eskimo village), boring its way seaward in a turmoil of spray and rising steam. Immediately in front of us it ran smoothly, soundlessly and with hardly a ripple. But about twenty yards to our right it disappeared through the wall of the fumarole, vanished into the mouth of a vast subterranean tunnel. And it was from this tunnel that the booming and roaring echoed out: great waves of tortured sound. We inched our way forward over the steam-misted rocks until we could peer into the tunnel. Straight into the mouth of hell.

"My God!" I whispered.

It was a terrifying scene. For thirty or forty yards down the tunnel the river ran straight; then came a right-angled bend; and at the bend a vast frenetic whirlpool had been scoured out of the rock: dark rings of water racing round and round in ever-tightening circles, until with a great roar they collapsed into the final terrifying vortex: a jet-black orifice plunging down into the very bowels of the earth: a fitting gateway to the horrors of the underworld.

As our eyes grew more accustomed to the dark we were able to take in details. The approaches to the whirlpool looked easy enough: for along either side of the tunnel the rocks were terraced up in a series of near-parallel ledges, and it looked like an easy scramble right up the lip. But how to get past the whirlpool itself? It looked impossible. For the water went racing round almost to the level of the roof, and the rock ledges had been scoured to a pristine smoothness.

We crouched together for some minutes, staring at the mouth of hell with a sort of horrified fascination; and after a while I noticed what looked like a series of footholds, cut into the rock round the whirlpool's farther rim. I pointed these out to Ross; and we agreed that they

146

might, conceivably, afford a way round—although how we got across the river to reach them we couldn't imagine.

We spent some time searching for a way across; but the poor light hampered us. We did see what looked like a rope hanging from the roof of the tunnel, but the end of it —if indeed it was a rope—was attached to the farther bank; and after we had both of us lost our footing and come near to toppling into the river—which would certainly have been the end of us—we agreed to go back and seek guidance from Freyja.

We found her and Somerville exactly where we had left them. And very relieved they were to see us: especially Freyja, who appeared to have thought that the moment we looked into the mouth of hell some terrible fate would have overtaken us. We sat on the floor of the fumarole discussing what to do next.

I judged it was well into the afternoon by this time: too late for further exploring. I therefore suggested that our next step ought to be to bring down our stores from the rim of the crater. After some discussion it was agreed that Ross and Somerville should stay by the river, while Freyja and I climbed back to the sledge and collected the most urgently nedeed of our supplies; an arrangement which suited me very well, since it gave me the chance of talking to Freyja about finding a way past the whirlpool.

Climbing the fumarole was far easier than descending it had been—for one thing we could see the holds instead of having to feel for them (since our bodies didn't screen off the light which came flooding in from above in great uninterrupted swaths); and in less than ten minutes we were out of the shaft and scrambling up the bowl of the crater. Above us we could see the sledge, just as we had left it, the dogs sheltering from the wind behind an outcrop of rock.

Now I had no forebodings as we clambered up: no premonitions of disaster. Not until the stone. The solitary loose stone came clattering down the terraces of rock.

We pulled up short. A sunset wind stirred the snow at our feet. Everything seemed suddenly very quiet. For a second time hung suspended—as in a room where a clock that has been ticking suddenly stops—then beside me I heard Freyja give a queer half-strangled gasp. And a second later the crater was alive with men—the men with yellow hair:

twenty or thirty of them, swarming out from among the boulders and rocks that lined the rim of the crater. From every point of the compass they closed in on us. The light of the dying sun shone on their clubs: blood-red.

14

"My Son, My Son"

WE were trapped. There was only one possible way of escape. I spun Freyja round.

"Quick!" I gasped. "Back to the fumarole."

But she slumped into the snow. Limply. Her voice was
toneless, like an automaton's. "We've broken the taboo,"
she said. "Now we must die."

I yanked her up. I shook her. Roughly. Till the numb-
ness went out of her eyes.

"We're not dead yet," I shouted. "If you want to see
Donald again, run."

And I half-tumbled, half-dragged her back to the fumarole.

We slid down the shaft in a cascade of debris, with the
nearest of the men with yellow hair less than a dozen
yards behind. Desperately we clawed our way from rock-
hold to rock-hold. Too much haste, a missed foothold, and
we'd crash three hundred feet to the rock below; too much
caution, too little speed, and we'd have our brains bashed
out by the whalebone clubs. It was a nice choice! Fragments of ice and rock, dislodged in our panic-stricken
scramble, went slithering down the walls of the fumarole;
we could hear, far below us, the continual splash-splash-
splash as they cascaded into the river.

"Ross! Somerville!" I shouted. "The men with yellow hair! Get your guns!"

The echoes flew from wall to wall, repeated, broken up, distorted. But the gist of the message got through. Below us we heard the sound of running: hobnail boots on the rocky floor of the fumarole. Then a reassuring shout.

"All right. We see you."

I took a quick look up. The men with yellow hair were streaming after us into the fumarole. But they seemed to be taking their time—they obviously reckoned they had us cornered, and there was no point in taking risks. At all events, by the time we'd slithered and scrambled down to level ground the nearest of our pursuers was still less than halfway down. Gasping and panting we stumbled across the rocks to where Ross and Somerville had taken up their positions, beside the river and just inside the mouth of the subterranean tunnel. Somerville pulled us under cover, and Ross raised his rifle.

"We can pick 'em off from here," he muttered. "One at a time."

For a moment I was too winded to speak. I lay on the rocky floor, panting and retching. Then I realized what he had said.

"No!" I gasped. "Don't shoot."

But it was too late.

The rifle cracked, and the foremost of the Eskimoes jerked away from his handhold. He gave one terrible piercing scream. In mid-air he did a complete slow-motion somersault. Then his body plummeted, with hardly a splash, into the river.

Even before he hit the water the crescendo of sound had begun to build up, as, in the confined space of the fumarole, the report of the rifle was flung from wall to wall and back again. Crack crack crack, the reports built up, like the lash of so many elephant whips, each louder and more vicious than the one before.

Then it happened.

A deeper, even more ear-splitting crack, and one of the sheets of hanging ice split away from the rock. With a shattering roar it collapsed on to the floor of the fumarole. There was a second of shocked silence. A high-pitched wail of terror from the Eskimoes. Then, one after another, all round the fumarole—like a 'berg split by the ring of a high-pitched note—the ice walls came crashing down.

We flung ourselves back into the tunnel as thousands of tons of ice and rock came pouring towards us. We saw the walls of the fumarole quiver like ill-set jelly; we saw great fissures leap like lightning from top to base of the walls of rock; then a seething avalanche piled up across the mouth of the tunnel, shutting out the scene of terror as behind us the whole of the fumarole—rock and ice and snow—came cataracting down.

Above us the roof of the tunnel quivered. Dust poured down from every fissure and crack. The rocks ground together, groaning like ship's timbers under unbearable strain. I thought, for several seconds, that they too were about to give way. Then at last the noise died: died to the rattle of an occasional boulder, rolling down in the wake of the tumult. And we were left standing, huddled together and trembling, in a world that was suddenly very still and very dark.

Our first reaction was one of relief: relief for a merciful escape. It was some little while before the full implication of what had happened came home to us. The graveyard of the whales, so everyone said, had only one entrance; that was blocked now; and we were inside it.

We sat down on the edge of what a few minutes before had been a deep fast-flowing river but was now a waterless runnel—for the avalanche had not only sealed us in, it had sealed the water out. For some time we were too shocked to speak. Then Somerville struck a match, and in its faint glimmer of light we began to examine the great bank of rock—thousands if not millions of tons of it— which lay between us and the outside world. After a few minutes' peering and probing it was obvious that we stood no more chance of breaking through than a mouse of scratching into the vaults of the Bank of England. We turned our attention to our rucksacks and pockets, making a little pile of all that was left of our worldly possessions. We found that we had a rifle, a Sten gun, and a couple of belts of ammunition; we had all our navigational equipment—compasses, sextant, chronometer and maps (which Somerville invariably carried in his rucksack wherever he went); we had our water-bottles (full); one box of matches (half-full); about a dozen sticks of solid fuel; two knives; one small ice-axe; some six or seven pounds of caribou cuts; a quarter of a tin of cocoa; and the clothes we stood up in. Everything else had been left on the sledge.

Well, there was obviously no future in sitting on the bed of the dried-up river. Our one hope was to push on: past the whirlpool, and into the graveyard. I handed round the sticks of solid fuel, which, when lit, made very passable candles. Then I turned to Freyja.

"You and I'll go first," I told her. "To show the others the way."

She didn't answer. She simply moved off like a sleep-walker along the bed of the runnel. In the guttering light of the candles her shadow, unnaturally erect, moved stiffly along the walls of rock. I moved up alongside her.

"You all right, Freyja?"

She said nothing. Her face was expressionless—as if she were in a trance; and her hand, when I took it, was cold: cold as ice. I realized that the events of the last hour must have been even more terrifying for her than for us. For while we saw the avalanche as a natural disaster, sparked off by a perfectly logical cause, she, no doubt, saw it as the wrath of the gods—a punishment meted out to those who had dared to defy their taboo and look into the mouth of hell. Small wonder she had been so shocked that her mind was completely numb. Small wonder, too, that as we approached the mouth of hell, her fear had built up to such a climax that she was like a sleep-walker—lost in another world: a world that was full of terrors beyond our comprehension. I kept hold of her hand: tightly.

We crossed the bed of the river (I learned later that the Shamen used to cross by swinging themselves over by ropes suspended from the tunnel roof; but more of this in its proper place). We scrambled up the farther bank. Then, along a series of roughly cut steps, we approached the whirlpool. And as we neared it, I caught some of Freyja's fear. For even with the river dried up, it was an awesome place: made more awesome by the uncertain light of our candles, which flickered and flared in the draught, now throwing the walls of rock into glittering relief, now plunging them into expected dark.

The whirlpool itself was of vast dimensions, at least a hundred feet across, I'd say, and two hundred feet in

152

depth. It was formed at a right-angled bend in the river where (as I afterwards learned) the influx of the incoming tide joined in diurnal battle with the outward flow of the river. Here, in the confined space of the subterranean tunnel, the seething waters had scoured a devil's cauldron out of the rock: a smooth inverted funnel, the brink of which we now skirted warily along a narrow ledge of rock. At first the going was reasonably easy, but after a while the ledge tapered away, and we were left clinging like flies to a series of foot- and hand-holds cut into the polished rock. We edged forward, inch by inch, every now and then staring down with a sort of fascinated horror into the vortex: a great inverted chimney, black and mysterious, spiralling down to apparently bottomless depths. At least, it would be truer to say that Ross, Somerville and I stared at the vortex. Freyja kept her eyes averted. I had a horrible premonition that her fear would be her undoing: that in her anxiety not to look down she would miss her footing and go slithering into the whirlpool—and a slip would have been a certain death, for the rock face was smooth as marble, worn to a highly polished sheen by the continual swirl of water.

But she didn't slip. None of us slipped. We edged ourselves on, inch by painful inch. And at last the footholds led on to a narrow ledge, and the narrow ledge, in turn, led round the last segment of the whirlpool and into the tunnel beyond. Thankfully, we scrambled back into the bed of the river. The whirlpool mouth of hell was behind us. It had all been easier than I had dared to hope.

I looked at Freyja. She was trembling; but after a while she began to lose her pallor and her frightening rigidity. I let go her hand.

"It's all right, Freyja," I said. "We got past. And you didn't look down."

She nodded, licking her lips. She ran her fingers over the rock; she traced a pattern in the sand with her toe; she could hardly believe she was still alive.

After a short rest to regain our breath and composure, we started off down the bed of the river, which, Freyja assured us, did indeed end up in the graveyard—although just how long it would take us to reach its mouth she didn't seem to know.

It was a strange journey. On either side the rock walls

rose steep and smooth; above us the roof was a mass of shadow; beneath our feet the bed of the river seemed to consist of alternate belts of rock and sand, so that our footfalls rang out unevenly, now loud and clear, now muffled and slurred. We groped our way forward in silence, mile after mile. At the end of some twenty minutes our first lot of candles burnt out. I decided not to light the others, but to keep them in case of emergency. In the pitch darkness that ensued our progress dropped to a crawl. We kept bumping into projections of rock; outcrops jutting out from the walls, protuberances rising up from the floor. The bed of the river twisted and turned; it was like a snake; it had no beginning and no end; it wound on and on and on. Eventually, worn out with fatigue, we called a halt, and shared round the little food we had in our rucksacks and drank a third of the water we had in our water-bottles.

As I was munching the last of my caribou cut, I suddenly noticed that my feet felt damp. I couldn't understand this; for the bed of the river, up to now, had been dry.

"Strike a match," I said to Somerville, "and let's have a look at the deck."

The light of the flame was small: a pin-point of brightness in an ocean of dark. But it was enough to confirm my fears. There was water on the bed of the river: a thin veneer of water. And I could guess how it got there. It was the advance guard of the rising tide. Even as the flame snuffed out I could see a new ripple coming slowly towards us along the floor of the tunnel. Millimeter by millimeter the water-level was rising.

"Freyja! How long before we're out of the tunnel?"

She shook her head. "I'm not sure. I think maybe one hour. Maybe two."

I turned to Somerville. "You're the best climber. Shin up the wall if you can. See if there's a high-water mark."

We lit a candle, and with much scrabbling and scrambling the professor disappeared into the darkness above us. A couple of minutes and he was down again. His voice was frightened.

"There's no high-water mark. The roof of the tunnel's damp."

We stood irresolute. If we went on, we'd be plunging

154

into deeper and deeper water. If we went back, we'd eventually find ourselves pinned by a rising tide against the wall of the collapsed fumarole.

"Come on," I grunted. "Let's get out of this."

And we went splashing down-river. Fast.

But, fast as we went, the water deepened faster. A hundred yards and it was up to our ankles: two hundred yards and it was not far short of our knees.

"Looks like we'll soon be swimming," I muttered.

Then came a merciful respite. The bed of the river widened; and for a while the water-level remained constant. We went splashing through the shallows, spurred on by an unspoken fear. For a time we made good progress. Then —as I had feared it was bound to—the tunnel narrowed, and the water-level rose. Soon it was up to our waists.

"Watch out for shafts in the roof," I panted. "Maybe there's a way up."

We lit a candle (Somerville, thank heavens, he had the sense to transfer the matches to his breast-pocket). In the guttering light we peered anxiously at the roof of the tunnel. It was smooth and unbroken. There were no shafts: no convenient chimneys into which we could crawl.

We walked on.

Inch by inch the water rose, over waists, armpits, and shoulders. Soon the candle was tossed aside, and we were swimming: swimming for our lives against the grey, insidious tide. As we struck out I noticed that Ross was still hanging on to his rifle.

"Leave it," I spluttered.

He let go of it thankfully; and it sank in a little thread of bubbles to the bed of the river not far from where, a few seconds before, I had dropped the Sten gun.

We swam on through the ever-deepening water. Soon we were out of our depth.

We swam on in single file, close to the wall of the tunnel—for here the tide flowed less strongly, and we could, when we became exhausted, cling to projecting ledges of rock.

We swam on through the darkness, like rats battling their way through the depths of an endless sewer.

We swam on and on until our muscles ached, our limbs felt like bollards of lead, and our breath came gasping out in short asthmatic pants.

We swam on and on until the water-level rose so high that we were swimming close to the roof of the tunnel. We knew then that soon, very soon, the whole of the subterranean passage would be a mass of water: the air space would be obliterated; a few despairing gulps of water and air, a few bubbles clinging to the last hollows in the roof, and we would be drowned.

I wasn't prepared for a death like this, fighting a last despairing battle for breath in the darkness under the earth. In the light of the sun and the smell of the sea I am (I like to think) no more of a coward than the next man. But I was a coward now: afraid, desperately afraid, not so much of the actual prospect of death as of the manner in which I was going to meet it. My arms flailing the water in a panic-stricken trudgeon, I began to forge ahead of the others. Then, rounding a bend in the tunnel some dozen yards in the lead, I pulled up short. Treading water, I stared downstream in amazement.

As the others came splashing round the bend, they too drifted to a surprised halt; and in a silent circle we trod water, breathing heavily, staring at the curtain of burnished silver which, some hundred yards ahead, appeared to stretch right across the tunnel, barring our path.

It rose like a wall of flame out of the dark water. Its light was unbelievably bright (like the cascading white of a magnesium firework); and it burned with a steady luminous glow. We swam cautiously towards it. It gave off no sound, no heat, no movement, simply the steady silver glow. And suddenly, in a wave of almost unbearable relief, I realized what it was. The moon. The silver moon, shining straight in through the mouth of the subterranean river.

"Come on!" I shouted. "We're through!"

And out of the subterranean tunnel we threshed our way thankfully into the moonlight. Gasping and spluttering, we heaved ourselves on to the rocks beside the mouth of the river. For several minutes we lay there panting and trembling, dripping great pools of water. Then we got slowly to our feet. The underground river and all its horror was behind us now. Ahead was our goal: the goal we had come so far and through so many strange and terrible vicissitudes to find: the legendary graveyard of the whales.

It lay in front of us bathed in moonlight: a woodcut in

ebony and silver, its outlines sharply defined: the towering mass of the cliffs, the narrow strip of sand ridged here and there with jagged outcrops of rock, and—strangest of all —the close-packed carcasses of the whales, scattered along the shore like the hulks of a derelict fleet. And what a vast number of carcasses there were! They lay in their hundreds if not in their thousands—Grey and Bowhead and Sperm, Beluga, Narwhal and White-beaked—in places so close together that one great carcass lay half-athwart the next. And, to my astonishment, every one of them appeared to be in good condition.[1] I was trying to puzzle this out when Ross, standing close beside me, gave a sudden gasp. He caught hold of my arm, so tight I nearly cried out.

"Look! A hut!"

He pointed to the shadows beneath the cliff some hundred yards from where we were standing.

The light of the moon played queer tricks, exaggerating each ridge and protuberance, turning each valley and hollow into a pool of darkness. In the kaleidoscope of ebony and silver quite a number of rocks took on strange shapes, some like crouching monsters, some like towering futuristic buildings. I thought at first that Ross's "hut" was one of the latter, a building of shadows, a creation of light and shade. But as my eyes became more accustomed to the moonlight, I began to wonder. It was a solid-looking and very three-dimensional building. From where we stood it looked exactly like a patchwork shelter of driftwood and rock, backing up against the base of the cliff. And the more we looked at it, the more solid it became. Hope surged up. Was the miracle really going to happen? Was the thousand-to-one chance really going to pay off? Could it be that not only were Somerville and I going to find our ambergris, but that Ross, against all the odds, was going to find his son?

[1] It often puzzled me afterwards why there was so little smell in the graveyard and why all the carcasses were in such excellent preservation. This I eventually discovered was due to two factors. (I) The very low temperature which acted as a refrigerant. (II) The fact that a strong westerly current flowed through the bay, and that every high tide the dead whales were refloated and carried by the current so much farther along the shore until they eventually reached and were sucked into the mouth of the underground river. Thus was the Eskimo legend fulfilled and the graveyard kept uncrowded. K. R.

In the doorway of the hut the shadows moved. And for a second the figure of a man was silhouetted clearly in the light of the moon.

"Donald! Donald!" The great shout echoed across the bay, and the captain began to stumble towards the shelter.

Somerville and I hung back. We wanted him to be the first to reach his son.

But he wasn't the first. Beside us a sudden flurry of movement. And Freyja, too, was rushing headlong towards the shelter. She outstripped Ross, and with a great cry of "Freyja!" the moonlit figure stumbled out of the doorway and into her arms.

The captain pulled up short. For perhaps ten seconds he stood motionless: rigid: as if carved out of rock. I heard him whisper four words: "My son, my son." Then, very slowly, he walked on towards the shelter.

In the doorway Freyja and Donald Ross were lost to the world, locked in each other's arms. Then the boy noticed his father.

"Dad!" he gasped. "This is too much." And overcome with shock and weakness—he was pitiably thin and emaciated—he fell fainting to the sand.

The girl knelt down. She raised his head; she crushed it against her breasts. As the three of us came towards her she looked up at us defiantly. "Keep off." The warning was clear. "He is mine."

15

The Guardians

WE sat outside the shelter and talked till the stars grew pale and the still white light of dawn came stealing across the bay. We were desperately tired; but there was so much to say, so many explanations to give, so many stories to tell.

Young Ross's, I think, was the most amazing story of all.

He filled in details, first, of the part we already knew: the flight to Prince Patrick Island, the blizzard, the crash landing, his life among the Eskimoes (who had apparently spared his life on account of his fair hair—the only other people to have set foot on the island, being Eskimoes, had naturally all been dark-haired). Then came the part we didn't know.

Following Freyja's directions he had come down through the underground river and arrived at the graveyard. He had found the ambergris—"Yes," he said, "it's here by the ton"—and had collected samples to take back with him to prove his story. He had planned to return to the Eskimo village, join up with Freyja and then, with her, make a dash by sledge for Winter Harbour. But things hadn't worked that way. For on his way back up the underground river he had slipped, breaking his leg. What he must have suffered in the next few months I shudder to think. Somehow, he told us, he had managed to drag himself back to the graveyard and to set the broken leg in splints of whalebone. Then he had waited, hoping that in time it would mend. But the leg hadn't mended; it had remained broken, useless and unbelievably painful. He had tried to crawl back along the tunnel, but each time he had failed to get past the whirlpool; and so eventually he had had no option but to settle down in the graveyard. He hadn't, to start with, either desired or expected to last very long. But death had proved perversely unwilling to claim him. His leg, though it got no better, also got no worse: a fresh-water spring in the cliffs kept him supplied with water; the whales and a species of seaweedy lichen kept him supplied with food. And he had lived on: day after day, week after week, month after month.

"But why," I interrupted, "didn't the Shamen come after you? They must surely have guessed you'd come to the graveyard."

He laughed.

"I took precautions. On the way down I burnt the ropes they use to swing themselves over the river. All but one. And that one I left on the graveyard side!"

He went on to tell us how, after he'd been in the graveyard a couple of months, in order to give himself something to do, he had started to collect ambergris—more to alleviate his boredom than in the hope of ever being able to use it. "Yes," he said in answer to my query, he had collected "quite a nice little pile." And helped by Freyja —who never left his side—he led us round to the back of the shelter.

It was more than a "little pile" he showed us; it was a mountain: a mountain of undreamed-of wealth: fabulous as the strikes on the El Dorado. When I saw it my throat went dry. It was several minutes before I could speak. Imagine yourself brought suddenly face to face with a heap of solid gold about ten feet high and twenty feet in diameter; well, that was the size of the pile of ambergris, and I knew it was worth every penny as much as gold. I knelt down and ran my fingers over the hard, oily lumps of mucus. They were smooth and cool, heavy and slate-grey in color, the very finest quality, worth at least £6 an ounce.

160

"There's enough in this one pile," I whispered at last, "to make every man jack of us millionaires."

"And I'd trade the lot," Somerville grunted, "for a set of Alpine climbing equipment!"

"Why?" Donald was puzzled—we hadn't told him about the rock fall yet. "You can easily haul it back up the fumarole."

My eyes met the captain's. There was no point in postponing telling him the truth; and I explained, as gently as I could, what had happened: that the fumarole was blocked: that the most obvious way of escape was sealed off. "But," I added cheerfully, "there are five of us now. And you can be sure of one thing. We'll soon find another way out."

He took it quite calmly: just reached for Freyja's hand and said, "So that's it. Now we're five."

I didn't take his pessimism too seriously. "I've been thinking," I said slowly, "if we can't get away by climbing the cliffs, we'll get away by sea. We'll build a boat."

He smiled, a resigned, unhappy smile. "Well, think again, Keith."

"Why? We've the raw material." I pointed to the carcasses of the whales.

But he shook his head. "We'll not get away by sea," he said. "And that's flat."

We asked him why. But by this time the stars had vanished and a morning breeze was coming in with the tide. We were none of us sorry when he said, "It's a long story. I'll tell you after we've slept."

It wasn't until we started to doss down that we realized how completely played out we were. Then, one after another in the most surprising attitudes, we dropped straight off to sleep: Ross with one boot on and one boot off, and Somerville in the middle of helping himself to snuff. I was just thinking how comic they looked, when, as I was rolling my anorak into a pillow, I too fell suddenly into a deep and dreamless sleep: the sleep of the utterly exhausted.

When I woke it was late afternoon, with the sun well down in the west. Of the others, Ross was still asleep; close beside me Somerville was stretching and yawning (evidently he too had just woken): and Freyja and Don-

161

ald were nowhere in sight. For a while I lay quietly on my side, scanning the shore, drinking in the strangeness of our surroundings; then I realized that I was extremely hungry. So, it seemed, was Somerville; and the two of us got up and entered the hut in search of food. We found a pile of whale cuts; a heap of seaweedy lichen, and enough oil to fry a banquet. In the far corner of the hut a shale fire was smouldering quietly, and before long we had concocted and eaten a meal which if not delicious, was none the less hot and nourishing.

Then we set out to have a closer look at the graveyard.

We walked down to the shore, picking our way in and out among the dead whales. I examined them eagerly; quite a good percentage of them were Sperm; but Somerville—to my surprise—seemed strangely disinterested. He replied to my queries and observations with nods and grunts. He was preoccupied. Then, as we came down to the water's edge, he said abruptly, "I'm worried about Ross. He'll take this hard."

I knew what he was getting at; but I shied away from an issue I didn't like.

"He's lucky to find his son at all," I grunted. "He oughtn't to mind sharing him."

"But he *will* mind."

I shrugged.

"Things will sort themselves out," I said. "Anyhow, it's their affair, not ours."

Looking back, I am shocked at my insularity: appalled at my self-centered obtuseness. I ought, of course, to have realized that the relationship between Freyja, Donald and Captain Ross was not an issue we could push on one side as "no business of ours"; it was something that concerned us all. Vitally. But then it is easy to be wise after the event. I did notice at the time that Somerville was looking at me with a curious intentness, as though he hoped I wasn't going to leave things at that. But I saw no reason to oblige him.

"Come on," I said. "Let's not look for trouble. Let's look for a way out of this damned graveyard." And I set off briskly along the shore.

In the center of the bay the beach was quite broad, but towards the horns it narrowed: degenerated into a twenty-foot strip of shingle overhung by towering cliffs. Now overhanging cliffs had an unhappy association for us, and we kept as far away from them as we could, paddling along by the edge of the water. We had gone only a few hundred yards when we heard an excited shout, and, looking back, saw Freyja and Donald running towards us, close to the foot of the cliffs.

"Keith! Somerville!" The boy's voice was frightened. "Get away from the water."

I couldn't see any danger.

"What's the panic?" I called back.

"For God's sake don't argue. Just get out of it. Quick."

His voice was urgent.

Better the devil you know, I thought, than the devil you don't. Keeping a wary eye on the cliffs, we scrambled back up the beach.

"What's the panic?" I repeated as we met midway between cliff and sea.

"I'll show you. The sooner you know, the better."

I looked back at the sunlit waters of the bay. They were serene and innocent, with currents and undertow no fiercer than on a pleasure beach. It was hard to see what danger could lurk in so untroubled a setting.

"I'll show you," Donald continued, "why I said last night that we'd never get out by sea."

He led us back past the shelter—where we picked up Captain Ross, who had been woken by the shouting—then along the beach to a point where a great outcrop of rock jutted into the bay. The four of us followed him down the outcrop, making for its seaward tip. I wondered what on earth we were going to see.

"Keep to the middle," Donald warned us. "Keep well away from the water."

I noticed that Freyja was for ever looking down at the sea and licking her lips. After a while she reached for Donald's hand.

At last we came to the end of the outcrop, which terminated in a great flat-topped rock jutting out from the end of the main formation rather like a landing-stage tacked on to the end of a break water. From here we had a magnificent view. Looking back we could see behind us the whole arc of the cliffs, falling sheer as a drop curtain into the bay; while ahead lay a vista that was scarcely less spectacular—the battleground of warm water and ice. I have already pointed out, I think, that the inner part of the bay was ice-free, whereas the outer part was ice-coated. But such a bare statement of fact gives little idea of the vast scene of conflict where ice and clear water met. For their meeting-ground was an ever-shifting kaleidoscope of floes and channels, as warm water from the underground river thrust seaward, only to be hemmed in and gradually congealed; while at the same time ice from the pack thrust inland, only to be thinned down and eventually melted; so that the sea, over an area of several square miles, resembled an ever-shifting mosaic of ice leads. It was a scene I could have watched, fascinated, for hours; but it wasn't, I knew, what young Ross had brought us to see.

He stood on the edge of the flat-topped rock scanning the sea lanes, shading his eyes against the glare of the sun.

"Look!" He pointed to the far side of the bay.

In the open water beneath the cliffs something moved: an alien fleck of black in a seascape of blue and white. As we watched, the fleck came towards us. Fast. It was joined by others, ten or twelve fast-moving splinters of black which came swirling out from among the sea lanes like iron filings drawn to a magnet. Then, in a wedge-shaped mass, they came swiftly towards us.

"Keep back!" I spoke sharply, for I had seen what the flecks were. Killer whales: *Orcinus orca:* the wolf pack of the Arctic: the most ferocious of all created animals. In a flurry of spray they came swirling up to the rock on which we were standing. They could see us, but they couldn't reach us. Angrily they darted to and fro some twenty feet below us. Then one of them jumped, jumped clean out of the water. For a second it hung in mid-air, its great jaws aslobber, then it plummeted back into the sea. Others followed suit. Again and again they leapt like great porpoises along the face of the rock, their jaws snapping like bear-traps, their small pig-like eyes agleam with angry malevolence. Freyja couldn't bear to look at them; she cowered back, covering her eyes.

Killer whales, I ought perhaps to explain to the uninitiated, are the most loathsome of all created creatures, hated and feared by all who come into contact with them. They are not true whales at all, but are misnamed dolphins, thirty feet in length, twenty-five to thirty tons in weight, and with three dozen wickedly pointed teeth, each eight inches long and sharp as a surgeon's scalpel. They also have the delightful trait of invariably attacking anything edible on sight—I once saw a pack of them kill and devour a hundred-foot Blue in less than a couple of minutes.

It was clear now why Donald had warned us away from the water: clear, too, why he had said we'd never get out by sea.

"Watch!" He pointed to the Killers. They had formed into a solid phalanx now, and were cruising slowly along the base of the rock. Suddenly in a great flurry of foam they shot seaward, heading straight for the ice pack. I couldn't think what they were after. Then I saw. Slowly down one of the sea lanes there drifted a carcass, the carcass of a great eighty-ton Sperm.

The Killers hit it before it was clear of the ice. We heard the thud of their jaws; again and again and again. The water was dyed red, a dark viscous red; and in front of our horrified eyes the mighty carcass was torn to shreds, was reduced in a couple of minutes to a skeleton of baleen and bone.

"Freyja's people call them the Guardians." Donald's voice was grim. "They act the part of Cerberus: watchdogs of hell."

"How many of them are there?" I asked.

"Three packs; fifteen to twenty in each. And," he added, "they spot anything that goes in *or out* of the bay."

We stood in silence, staring at the Killers. Slowly the utter hopelessness of our predicament came home to us. Our last avenue of escape was blocked. We couldn't climb the cliffs; we couldn't get back up the underground river; we couldn't escape by sea. We were sealed in: lost to the world as surely as if we had been marooned on the farthest star in the firmament.

Somerville helped himself to snuff. He was surprisingly calm. "It looks," he said matter-of-factly, "as if we've jumped out of the frying-pan into the fire."

Young Ross began to limp up and down. "We might be worse off," he said. "We've plenty of water, and plenty of food. And," he looked at Freyja, "we've a lot to be thankful for."

The professor smiled. " 'A Jug of Wine,' " he said, " 'a

165

Loaf of Bread—and Thou beside me in the Wilderness . . .' "

"What are you drooling about?" The captain's voice was sharp. "This isn't Paradise. This is Hell. And the sooner we find a way out the better."

His son smiled. *"You* find a way out," he said.

"Keith!" The captain appealed to me. "There *has* to be some way out?"

I thought of the ambergris: the fabulous pile of ambergris: a cool £3,000,000 worth.

"Yes," I said slowly, "there has to be some way out. And not empty-handed."

16

No Way Out

Our first step was to take stock of our resources.

We had plenty of water; for although the underground river had been warm, saline and quite unsuitable for drinking, a small fresh-water spring cascaded down the cliff about two hundred yards from the hut. "Cascaded" is perhaps rather too grand a word, for in dry weather the volume of water was hardly more than a trickle; but at least it never dried up.

Food was more of a problem. The whales, it is true, provided an inexhaustible supply of meat; but we lacked vegetables, and our only source of vitamin C was a sea-weed-like lichen which clung to the rocks. This, when boiled, had a most nauseating iodine taste; but beggars couldn't be choosers, and since the lichen probably saved our lives I suppose I shouldn't quibble about its flavor. Our only other sources of food were limpets, and a certain bitter berry (known, according to Somerville, as Salmon-berry, although anything less like salmon I have never tasted!). Our diet, in other words, was monotonous and none too well balanced, but it was enough to keep us alive.

Our other assets were the rocks of cliff and shore, among which was an oily shale—which burned steadily though with very little heat—and the whales, whose vast carcasses provided us with a veritable treasure trove.

Having satisfied ourselves that we could eke out an existence of sorts more or less indefinitely, we set about making a thorough survey of our surroundings. First, we explored the cliffs to the west. We examined them in detail, section by section and with the greatest care; but nowhere could we find the slightest hope of making an ascent. And when we tried to work our way along the cliff foot, we soon came to the point where the beach tapered completely away and the sea came lapping directly against the rock. And in the sea were the Killers. The moment we neared the water they came swirling up, hopefully, their great mouths aslobber. We beat a hurried retreat. Nor, when we came to explore the cliffs to the east, was the prospect any rosier. We couldn't climb up them; we couldn't work round them; nowhere, it seemed was there the slightest chink in the graveyard's defenses.

Ross and I were bitterly disappointed; but Somerville was philosophic. "Be patient," he admonished us. "We'll get out in the end."

Something in the way he said it made me look at him hopefully. "You thought of a way?"

He pointed to the sea. "Now the river's blocked," he said slowly, "there's no warm water coming into the bay. See what that means. There's nothing to stop the ice forming naturally, right up to the shore. If we wait, it'll soon be thick enough to stand on. Then we can walk straight out of the graveyard. Just like that!"

"That's always assuming," Donald Ross cut in, "that the river doesn't break through again."

The professor nodded.

Filled with renewed hope we hurried down to the water's edge. Somerville was right. If we hadn't been so busy surveying the cliffs we would have noticed it before. Already fragments of pack ice were beginning to nose their way into the bay: already a thin filmy veneer was forming on the water close inshore.

We slept soundly that night, buoyed up with renewed hope. And next morning the bay was coated in ice.

It wasn't very thick; in fact it was hardly more than a glaze (for salt water freezes far more slowly than fresh); but the little there was a symbol, a token of things to come. And all that day as the ice slowly spread and thick-ened our cheerfulness increased. The Killers, in contrast, were clearly very much put out by the sudden freeze-up of their hunting ground. We saw them threshing about, hour after hour, struggling to break the ice with their great triangular fins, blowing angrily as they were forced into ever-narrowing sea lanes. Then, a little before sunset, they started to fight.

What triggered them off we never discovered—though I suspect it was the fact that one pack was driven by the encroaching ice into another's territory—but whatever the cause, the outcome was a vicious panic-stricken battle which dyed the water scarlet and didn't end until the sur-vivors of the defeated pack had been driven on to the beach; here they threshed and flailed until the sun sank and the moon rose, and by morning they were stiff and lifeless as frozen fillets of cod.

As we passed them on our way to inspect the ice, we couldn't help shuddering at the sight of the great wounds which lacerated their bodies from snout to tail. We hoped that perhaps they had fought each other to extermination; but in this we were disappointed; for as we neared the beach we saw the survivors—some couple of dozen of them—circling a pool of open water about a hundred yards off shore. Round and round they went, blowing an-grily, splintering against the rim of the ice in a desperate struggle to keep open a last patch of water.

Keeping a wary eye on them, we tested the ice. It was a couple of inches thick: nearly thick enough to walk on. It seemed almost too good to be true.

"Another three or four days," I said, "and we'll be away."

And we began, that morning, to prepare for the long haul back to Winter Harbour. We started to stock-pile food, sufficient whale cuts and lichen to last us through the winter. We started work on a stretcher for young Ross, and eleven-foot skis (fashioned out of whale ribs) for the rest of us. And finally we set to work to build a sledge: a sledge that was big enough to take our food *and* a load of ambergris, and light enough for the four of us to be able to haul it across the ice.

There followed a period of feverish activity, all of us working flat-out in the hours of daylight, which seemed suddenly far too short. A few days of eager expectancy, with the ice thickening slowly but surely. Then the night of disillusion.

A little after midnight on our seventh day in the grave-yard we were shot out of our slumbers by the most appalling roar. Rushing into the open, we saw that about a mile along the beach a great landslip had taken place, a whole section of the cliff having toppled headlong into the bay. And that wasn't all. Long after the rumble of falling rock had died away, there persisted an angry, seething turmoil of sound: the sound of water, scouring its way through freshly fallen debris. There was no doubting what had happened. The underground river had burst its chains. Once again it was flooding into the bay. By dawn the ice would have gone.

An angry despair welled up inside of me. For a second I thought of rushing madly across the ice, of making a desperate dash for freedom before once again we were sealed irreparably in—condemned to a living death among the piled-up bodies of the Lost Ones. But even as the idea came to me I knew it was too late. As the warm water cascaded into the bay there was a hissing upthrust of steam; then a series of sharp reports, "crack crack crack," as the ice split into melting fragments.

We walked slowly back to the hut. Our despair was all the more bitter because our hopes had been so high.

We didn't sleep the rest of the night. We talked, cooked ourselves a meal and waited impatiently for dawn; and first light saw us hurrying down to the beach. Once there, our worst fears were confirmed. The warm-water river was pouring out through a hole in the cliff. The ice had melted. The Killers were cruising contentedly off shore.

We hoped at first that there might be a way up the landslip; but the more closely we examined it, the more obvious it became that we could never climb it. For the river had burst through about half-way up the cliff. It had burst through with such force that a great hole had been blasted clean out of the rock: a hole through which the river was now spurting like water agush from a pump. And there was no way we could reach this hole; for between it and the beach on which we stood was a drop of a good two hundred feet; sheer, and swept by the waterfall. We knew it was hopeless. But none the less we spent the

170

rest of the day poking and prying among the debris, struggling a few feet up the spray-drenched rock only, inevitably, to be brought up short.

By the time we got back to the hut we were depressed and exhausted.

We none of us talked much that night. But we thought a lot.

There are certain periods in everyone's life the memory of which one would give a good deal to be able to sponge away. Such a period was the five or six weeks after the landslip. It was, for all of us, a time of frustration and mounting despondency. For, try as we would, we could find no possible way of getting out of the graveyard. Neither toil nor daring nor ingenuity brought the slightest hint of reward. We were sealed in. And that was that.

We all of us took it differently. Donald and Freyja were the least perturbed; and if I had ever doubted the *cliché* that love is blind I learned the truth of it now, for I believe that the pair of them were actually happy! Somerville, as always, made the best of a bad job with the minimum of fuss, accepting our predicament with an almost Oriental passivity. Ross, on the other hand, became possessed of a feverish activity; he was ever engaged in hair-raising experiments, ever propounding elaborate and usually quite impractical schemes of escape. He had us, for example, driving whale-bone pitons up the face of the cliff—but not unnaturally the pitons broke; he had us probing the underground tunnel—but we found it blocked; and he had us trying to lure the Killers into lobster-pot-like traps—which was nearly the end of us all!

After this last fiasco the rest of us fought shy of his schemes. But this didn't deter him. He went on with them alone; and soon he was covering the back of every available chart with a mass of notes about the Killers' habits and routine. We didn't doubt he was planning another attempt; and in due course he came out with it; a night escape by boat.

The scheme he put forward was very simple. He had noticed, he told us, that there were two packs of Killers and each had their own territory. The pack in the west seemed to have no fixed routine, but the pack in the east had certain fixed habits. On calm moonlight nights, for example, they invariably left the shore and patrolled some mile to seaward close to the edge of the ice. This, Ross insisted, was a routine which was never broken; his notes (which he passed round) proved it; on certain nights the Killers *always* kept well clear of the shore.

"So," he ended, "we'll build a boat. We'll wait for a calm moonlit night. Then we'll row out of the graveyard, hugging the cliffs. It's as simple as that."

His scheme was not well received. We could all of us picture far too vividly what would happen if the Killers decided to change their routine. Freyja was especially against the boat. For to her the Killers were more than a pack of ferocious whales, they were the guardians of the graveyard, the watchdogs of hell; and she was convinced that if she went anywhere near the water they would tear her limb from limb—hadn't the Shamen prophesied the most terrible death for anyone who violated the graveyard's taboo?

I expected Ross to be angry at our lack of enthusiasm. But he wasn't. He took it as something he had anticipated; and that evening he insisted on our following him down to the beach. He had, he said, something to show us.

I had a sudden premonition of what was coming next.

"Don't do anything silly," I warned him.

He laughed.

Following his lead, we scrambled on to a projecting ledge a few feet up the face of the cliff. From here he pointed across the bay.

"See them?"

The night was cloudless, with a full moon blazing out of a velvet sky. To seaward the pack ice was sparkling like a necklace of diamonds, and following the line of Ross's outstretched finger we could see, silhouetted against it, the familiar flecks of black: the Killers, a pack of about fifteen, cruising slowly along the edge of the ice. They were roughly a mile offshore.

"Yes," I said. "We can see them."

"They'll stay there all night."

"Possibly," I said.

"Not possibly. Certainly."

"But they'd head for the shore soon enough," Somerville cut in, "if they saw anything move."

"They can't see as far as the shore."

"How do you know?" I asked him. "You can't be certain of that."

Ross laughed. "I've proved it once," he said, "to myself. Now I'll prove it again. To you." He started to strip off his clothes.

"There's no need," I said quickly, "for that. We'll believe you."

He took not the slightest notice.

"Dad!" Young Ross grabbed his father's arm. "No!"

The captain shook him off. Before any of us could stop him he had jumped off the ledge, had run across the beach, and was wading into the sea. A few paces and he was out of his depth; then he was swimming along the foot of the cliffs, about a dozen yards offshore.

I didn't know whether to look at Ross or the Killers. I felt certain they'd spot him, that they'd come swirling in to the shore, that in front of our eyes they'd tear him limb from limb. In spite of the cold I started to sweat; I could feel the dampness trickling out from under my armpits.

It happened suddenly. One second Ross was swimming quietly along, the next he was shouting and threshing and flailing at the water. The hair rose up on the nape of my neck. I felt sick with horror. It was several seconds before I realized he was doing it on purpose, that he was deliberately making as much noise—and more—as we would make in a boat. Beside me Somerville swore softly. Young Ross sat down, his face white. And the Killers stayed motionless beside the pack ice.

For a good ten minutes Ross swam up and down, splashing and singing. And when at last he came scrambling ashore I could hardly believe he was safe. He had, it seemed to me, tempted providence too flagrantly to deserve to get away with it. But he had proved his point. There was no denying that.

We walked back to the hut in an awkward, restrained silence. Then Somerville said simply, "What do you suggest we do?"

Ross smiled. "I suggest we build a boat," he said.

There was a long silence. I looked at Freyja. Her face

173

was expressionless; but I noticed the little droplets of sweat beading her forehead.

"What do you think, Donald?" I said.

If he had spoken out against the boat I think that I, at any rate, would have been willing—for the sake of Freyja —to drop the idea. But he didn't. Instead, he turned to the girl for help: gave her a "what do you think?" look. But she wouldn't help him. Her eyes refused to meet his.

Captain Ross was watching his son. "There's no risk, Donald," he said. "Haven't I just proved that?"

It was a cruel decision to have to make. For a long time he was silent; then, suddenly, he made up his mind.

"I think," he said—and his voice was strangely harsh and defiant—"I think the boat's worth a try."

As he said it he looked very straight at his father; but his eyes refused to meet Freyja's.

Next morning we set to work.

First we drew up plans. After much discussion we agreed to budget for a twenty-two-foot, broad-beamed rowing boat, built on much the same lines as a Naval whaler. The boat had to be big enough to take the five of us, plus ambergris and stores; it had to be light enough for us to row; and it had to be a hundred per cent seaworthy. An ambitious project: but then we all agreed that the boat-building was something which had to be tackled properly or not at all.

Next came the question of a building site. We couldn't start work high up on the beach, because from there the boat would be impossible to launch (once finished it would be far too heavy for us to move over the sand); and we couldn't start work at the water's edge because of the Killers. In the end it was Ross who hit on the solution.

"Let's," he said, "dig a dock at the side of the river. When the boat's finished we'll channel off enough water to float it down."

It was a good plan, but easier to make than to carry out. In the event it took us over a week to dig the dock— whalebone spades are never likely to scoop the market, for they blunt and snap with equal facility—but at last, after long hours of sweating and swearing, the pit was ready: thirty feet long, fifteen feet wide and four feet deep: and very proud of it we were.

Next, we collected together our materials. And it was here, of course, that we ran into trouble: for there were so many things that we were short of, so many gaps that not even Ross's ingenuity could plug. But after a fortnight of dismembering the nearby whale carcasses, experimenting, carting, hauling and stockpiling, we amassed round the perimeter of the dock quite an impressive array of material: about six tons of graded whale-ribs (between twenty and thirty feet long), about four tons of baleen (the long flexible strips of bone found in the roof of the whales' mouths and at one time much prized by corset makers), a large pile of "nails" (sharpened splinters of whalebone), a fantastic length of gut (gleaned from the whales' intestines), a pile of blubber and *grax* (which, when boiled, exuded a glue-like substance which was our nearest substitute to tar), and finally a large mound of shale—the raw material of heat. These, together with our knives and a few fragments of driftwood and reed, were all that we had to work with; and I must admit that to start with I was none too optimistic about getting the boat finished.

Nor would we have got it finished if it hadn't been for Ross. It was he who kept us at it; he whose inventiveness rescued us from each successive impasse; and he whose patience never failed in the days when progress was so infinitesimal that the rest of us felt like losing heart.

As it was, the keel, under his tireless guidance, gradually took shape rib by rib, the twenty-foot bands of whalebone being slotted into each other at stem and stern and bound together with gut. At the end of the third week we were ready to fit thwarts and rudder—for which we had set aside solid blocks of backbone. This took a further ten days; then the skeleton was complete. And very imposing it looked. Even Freyja by this time was showing signs of interest, if not of enthusiasm; and as for myself I must admit that as the boat progressed so my spirits rose in direct ratio. However, the longest and most difficult part of our task still lay ahead: giving the skeleton a watertight skin. By experiment we found that the thinner strips of baleen were very pliable and could be inserted in and out between the ribs rather like a weaver's warp. This we proceeded to do, weaving the baleen under and over the transverse struts like so many wicker-workers fashioning a

175

gargantuan basket. The work was laborious and painfully slow. But at least it was simple and after a while we fell into a comfortable routine. Each morning I would cut the baleen out of the mouth of the nearest whale, Ross and Somerville would drag it across to the dock, and Freyja and Donald would split and trim it into convenient lengths; then in the afternoon we would each of us "weave" a section of the boat. This routine we followed for five days a week. On the sixth day we "enjoyed"—if that is the right word—a grand glueing session. Early in the morning Freyja and Donald would stir up the fire, feeding it with dried reeds and blowing on it with our Heath Robinson bellows until the shale gave off its maximum heat. Then we would melt the blubber and *grax* (collected the night before), catching the exuded glue-like oil in whalebone pans, and smearing it liberally over our week's baleening. It was messy, back-breaking work; but the great thing was that the glue stuck fast; it sealed up the cracks in the baleen, giving the boat a first-rate waterproof veneer. Most of the seventh day we spent washing ourselves free from glue!

And so the weeks passed, quickly and almost pleasantly now that we had a purpose to which we could harness our energy. While the boat-building was in progress we didn't, of course, give up trying to find alternative ways out of the graveyard. But we could hit on no idea that held even the remotest prospect of success; and eventually I, at any rate, fell to pinning all my faith in the boat. It wasn't a case of deliberately putting all our eggs in one basket. It was a case of having only the single basket to put anything in . . .

As the weeks lengthened into months the days became shorter, the nights colder, and our bodies thinner—the result, no doubt, of our unbalanced diet. We also suffered a certain amount from lassitude—the result of the cold and the lack of vitamin C. Then, early in the New Year, we had a series of blizzards which put paid to boat-building. For sixteen days at a stretch we were confined to our shelter; and when at last the sky cleared, we had to dig both ourselves and our boat from under a ten-foot canopy of snow. I was afraid that the half-finished framework might have been crushed; but my fears were groundless. Whalebone is tough and resilient; not a strut had cracked, and soon we were back to our old routine: cutting and trimming, weaving and glueing.

And at last, almost exactly three months after we'd laid the keel, the boat was finished.

17

"Greater Love Hath No Man Than This . . ."

WE WERE determined to leave nothing to chance. Every eventuality we discussed *ad nauseam:* every precaution that it was possible to take we took with meticulous thoroughness. We tested the boat not once, but five times; and finding her slightly bow-heavy spent a full week trimming and lightening her stem-piece. We muffled the oars, we oiled the rowlocks, we collected powdered shale to darken our faces and hands, and finally we loaded up with stores.

What to take and what to leave behind was quite a problem. Too many stores and the boat would be impossible to row; too few, and if we did manage to land farther along the shore we would be unable to manage the journey back to Winter Harbour. In the end we agreed to limit ourselves to half a ton of ambergris (worth roughly £500,000), three hundredweight of whale-cuts (enough to last us a good two months), and two hundredweight of gut and baleen (the idea being that when we found a landing point we would put ashore, dismantle the boat, and use the gut and baleen to build a sledge). For several days we were busy stockpiling, experimenting, testing and load-

178

ing; then there was nothing we could do but wait: wait for a clear moonlit night.

It was while we were waiting that an incident occurred which showed how keyed up all of us were.

One evening I noticed that Freyja and Donald had been whispering together for some time with unusual seriousness in their own patent brand of Eskimo-cum-pigdin-English. I could tell that something important was being discussed; I could tell, too, that they were, for once, having difficulty in understanding each other. I wasn't therefore surprised when they called me in as an interpreter.

The trouble centered round Freyja's locket. She was, I gathered, trying to tell Donald something important about it; but just what it was he couldn't fathom. In the end I managed to get to the bottom of it. And a pathetic little story it was that I eventually wormed out of her.

The Shamen, you may remember, had invested the scent-filled lockets with a sort of religious significance; they had for years been drumming it into the fair-haired Eskimoes that unless they were buried with one of these lockets alongside them, they could never hope to enter heaven. It was this belief which now acted as a whetstone to Freyja's fear. For she was convinced that if she set foot in the boat, not only would the Killers tear her to pieces, but also that her locket would be lost along the sea lanes and that she would, in consequence, be denied all hope of ever going to heaven. And the terrible thing was this: her belief in the Shamen's teaching was so unquestioning, so deeply ingrained that there was no shaking it. Nothing that Donald and I said or did was any sort of comfort to her.

As I paced up and down, trying to think of some way of reassuring her, I thought I heard a sound from the far side of the rock behind which we'd been sitting. I walked round it quickly. And there was Captain Ross—ostensibly stacking up a pile of baleen. I wondered how much he had overheard. We stood and looked at each other. If I had accused him of eavesdropping, or if he had led off with excuses, it would have triggered a first-class row. As it was we just stood and stared at each other until at last I said:

"We're getting jumpy. The sooner we make a break for it the better."

He nodded. "Tomorrow," he said. "Provided the weather's okay."

Next evening the sea was calm as a dew-pond.

We pushed off at a few minutes to midnight.

The keel grated harshly on the sand; for a second the boat drifted broadside on, tugged at by current and undertow; then as Ross and I took the oars and Freyja the tiller, we steadied up. This was the moment for which we had planned and sweated and toiled these last three months. This was the moment of crisis.

From the second we got under way we could see the Killers quite clearly. They were keeping their usual station, close to the edge of the pack. To my overwrought imagination, they seemed to be more active than usual—to be cruising up and down with unwonted restlessness. But at least—thank God—they were showing no sign of coming inshore.

Rowing an easy unhurried stroke, and steering as close to the cliffs as we could, we headed along the curve of the bay. It was a quiet and very beautiful night, with a handful of gemlike stars and a great three-quarters moon, gold as a field of wheat; and, as we edged noiselessly along the shore, moon and stars came swimming along below us as well as above—reflected in exact detail in water as smooth and motionless as glass. We rowed in silence; Donald and Somerville in the bow, Ross and I amidships, our stores stacked up in the stern, and Freyja perched alongside the tiller. Our oars were muffled, our skin was daubed with shale—to deaden its whiteness, and the boat was soaked in whale oil—both to lessen friction and deaden creaks. Soon we were nearing the tip of the bay.

And here we had a stroke of luck; for the current increased in strength; it gave us a helping hand, so that we fairly shot round the headland with hardly a stroke rowed. From now on we were in unknown waters.

We steered close inshore, hugging the cliffs, looking for somewhere to land; but the cliffs, in a long unbroken line, fell sheer into the sea. And soon I was aware of two developments that I didn't like. Firstly, as we moved farther away from the warm-water river the sea grew progressively colder, and as a result the pack ice began to converge on the shore. Secondly, the Killers seemed to be keeping pace with us, to be moving parallel to us along the edge of the ice.

I counted them. Sixteen. Great streamlined battering rams of muscle and bone. They were so close that I could make out their individual markings: the piebald blotches of black and white, and the narrow riband of yellow curving from belly to snout. They were moving fast: were cruising up and down the edge of the pack in quick excited spurts. I couldn't think what was exciting them. Unless it was us . . .

I eased the stroke—a splash would have been fatal now. And we edged ever closer beneath the cliffs. I felt the sweat trickling down my back.

Then it happened.

A sudden commotion beside the ice: a pair of Killers breaking away from the pack: and two sail-like triangular fins sweeping towards us, fast. My mouth went dry. A terrible coldness flooded over me, as though I'd been plunged naked into an ice-cold shower. Then the Killers swung aside. And I saw—in a moment of unspeakable relief—that they had thoughts for other things than food. They were mating. We held our breath as they flashed past us, not fifty yards from the boat, in a flurry of playful pursuit. Soon they were out of sight.

Trembling, we rowed on.

And at long last we began to leave the Killers behind. Slowly, almost imperceptibly, the gap between us widened: one hundred yards, one hundred and fifty, two hundred. Soon we could see ahead of us a promontory beyond which the cliffs fell sharply away. Once round that we'd be out of sight; once out of sight we'd be safe. We rowed on: carefully, noiselessly, our expectation of life increasing with every stroke. Soon we were so close to the promontory that we could see at its base the little bubbles of foam where the ground swell sucked the sea away from the cliffs. Another thirty or forty strokes, I thought, and we'll be safe.

Then everything happened at once.

From the ice almost opposite where we were rowing (not fifty yards from the boat) came a sudden crack: and there, silhouetted in the silver light of the moon, were two great whale carcasses being squeezed out of the pack ice, like larvae forced from their chrysalis. A gasp of fear

181

from Somerville. I spun round and saw that the Killers were racing back, were swirling towards the carcasses in a solid, purposeful phalanx.

We froze, cowering back against the foot of the cliffs.

Like a flurry of cosmic thunderbolts the Killers tore into the foremost carcass. We could hear the thud, thud, thud of their jaws ripping great caverns out of the dead whale: fifty or sixty pounds of flesh with every slashing bite. The water, in a widening viscous pool, turned crimson.

Then—to my horror—I realized that the incarnadined pool was drifting shoreward. Propelled by current and tide, it was drifting straight towards us.

The others, too, saw what was happening. Ross's mouth fell open. "My God!" he meant to say—I could see the words trying to form—but all that came out was a strangled croak. Donald caught hold of Freyja's hand. Somerville's oar clattered to the deck. As for me, I was so petrified with terror that it was several seconds before I realized we had one chance, and one chance only. I grabbed an oar.

"Quick! Row for our lives!"

With a violent thrust I fended off from the cliff. Our oars bit deep into the water. And we rowed. Rowed as we had never rowed before, while after us drifted the carcasses, the widening pool of blood, and the Killers.

We pulled till our muscles cracked and the sweat poured out of our hair and into our eyes. But the boat was heavy—how I cursed the dead weight of ambergris which in my greed I'd insisted on bringing; but it was too late to jettison it now—and the Killers, circling and darting at the carcasses, kept easy pace with us.

Thirty or forty strokes and we were rounding the headland. Another few seconds and we'd have been safe. Then we were spotted.

Behind us the foremost of the Killers leapt high out of the water. In an evil Satanic sort of way, I suppose he was beautiful: a curving arc of iridescence, silhouetted against the moon, his eyes aglint like quartz, his mouth aslobber with blood. With hardly a ripple he knifed back into the water. Then he came after us: purposefully, fast.

With any other creature there might have been hope. But not with the Killers. For invariably, no matter what

182

the circumstances, they attack on sight. And they had all sighted us now. Like a pack of bloodhounds hot on the scent, they came tearing in for the kill.

We knew that only a miracle could save us. Yet we rowed on. Frantically. Desperately. And, as we rounded the headland, hope—for a second—welled up. For there in front of us lay an open beach: a shelving arc of shingle less than a hundred yards ahead. But the hope was stillborn. The hundred yards was too far. The Killers were closing too fast. We knew we would never make it. But we rowed on, with the blind unreasoning frenzy of the condemned.

Fifty yards from the shore and the Killers were on top of us. So this was the end. My mind went blank with horror. Yet I went on rowing mechanically; and I remember it distressed me almost beyond endurance that Ross was lagging a fraction of a second behind in his stroke.

Then Freyja dropped the tiller. She stood up. She pulled off her locket and flung it towards the shore. She looked at Donald Ross and I think she tried to smile.

"It is me they have come for," she whispered.

And before we realized what she was doing she had dived overboard. Straight in the path of the Killers.

I'll never forget the look on young Ross's face: the eyes too appalled to focus, the arm flung up in a vain attempt to blot out something too terrible to be seen. He tried to jump up; but his injured leg folded beneath him, and either from pain or horror or a combination of both he fainted, falling stiff as an epileptic across the thwarts.

Behind us a swirl of churned-up sea: a thud of jaws, and the Killers checking to thresh and fight over something unspeakable.

In the brief second of grace we rowed on: mechanically, our minds numb with horror. Then the keel was agrate on the shore.

We beached in a flurry of spray with the Killers again on top of us. At the very second we grounded one of them smashed into our stern, stoving it in like an eggshell. We flung ourselves on to the beach as inches behind us the Killers splintered the boat to matchwood. For a second Ross and I paused and looked back, as between us we dragged the unconscious Donald to safety. It was a pause that nearly cost us our lives. For one of the Killers leapt

183

at us: leapt clean out of the water and on to the beach.
We flung ourselves back as, on the spot where we had
stood only seconds before, the razor-sharp teeth churned
up the sand in angry frustration. We staggered away, panting, gasping and retching, and collapsed on the coarse grey
sand some twenty yards from the sea.

My heart was thudding in quick uneven spurts; in front
of my eyes the curve of the beach was undulating up and
down like a scenic railway; and I thought I was going to
faint. But at last, very slowly, my breathing began to return to normal and my vision to clear. And looking up I
saw that the captain was on his feet: was staring at the
water's edge. After a while I saw what he was staring at.

About two dozen yards to the right of our boat—now
splintered to matchwood—a small white object was bob-
bing merrily up and down, now borne inshore on the crest
of a wave, now tugged out by the undertow. It was
Freyja's locket.

Ross's eyes were fixed on it with preoccupied intentness.
He was breathing heavily. His fingers were clenching and
unclenching. Then, like a sleepwalker, he began to walk
down to the sea.

I scrambled to my feet. "No!" I shouted. "Don't be a
fool!"

He took not the slightest notice. His eyes were fixed on
the locket.

He chose his moment well: when, on the crest of a little
wave, the disc of whalebone came drifting close to the
shore. He leapt into the water. He picked it up cleanly,
with a smooth, well-judged sweep of his hand. Then he
dived for the beach. But quick as he was, the Killers were
quicker. Before he was clear of the water, two of them
sprang at him.

I covered my eyes. I heard a voice screaming in terror
—"No! No! No!"—I didn't recognize the voice as my
own. I didn't see what happened clearly; for as I stumbled
—sick with fear—towards the water's edge, sea and beach
and Killers and Captain Ross were whirling in front of my
eyes like the patterns of a kaleidoscope. But what happened, Somerville told me afterwards, was this. In their
eagerness to get at Ross two of the Killers collided in
mid-air. Their jaws slashed together. But not on Ross; on
each other; and he slid out, untouched, from under their

flailing bodies. Somerville and I grabbed him. We swung him clear; we dragged him back up the beach. Then, panting and trembling, we sank face-down on to the sand.

Later, a long while later, Ross sat up. I saw he was fumbling with the locket, was running his fingers round and round the polished whalebone. His face was withdrawn; expressionless. At last he got to his feet and walked slowly across to his son—who was still laid out unconscious at the foot of the cliff. Carefully he put the locket into his hand. Gently he folded his fingers, one by one, over the curve of the whalebone. Then he turned, and, shoulders hunched up, went walking along the beach. Beneath the towering cliffs he looked small and lost and insignificant: a papier-mâché silhouette dwarfed by the immensity of sea and rock and sky. I wanted to call him back, but Somerville shook his head.

"Leave him," he said. "He's best alone."

It took us twenty-four hours to salvage the ambergris and what was left of the whale cuts and stores. It was dangerous work—for even at low tide the Killers were unpleasantly near—but we got down to it with a will; glad to have something that helped take our minds off Freyja's death. I was quite surprised at the amount of food and material we were able to save.

Next day we explored our surroundings. We soon found that the cliffs were lower and far less precipitous than those of the graveyard; and after much reconnoitering and scrambling we managed to find a route to the top—a route up which we could take both the sledge and a stretcher for young Ross.

And a stretcher was going to be needed; there was no doubt about that. For Donald was in bad shape. His leg was twisted, swollen and excruciatingly painful; and (which was even worse) he had lost all interest in staying alive. He admitted this with a frightening detachment: life, he said, no longer held any interest for him: he hoped he was going to die. He lay on his back at the foot of the cliffs, hour after hour, day after day, his face beaded with sweat, his eyes listless and staring at things the rest of us couldn't see. And die he would have, if it hadn't been for his father.

I was amazed at the change in the captain. The old

185

drive and forthrightness were still there, but they were cloaked now by a new-found humility and a considerateness for others which had been noticeably lacking before. And he now settled down to look after his son with all the gentleness and attention to detail of a dedicated nurse. He sat beside him day and night, sponging the perspiration off his face, giving him courage when the pain of his leg goaded him almost beyond endurance, and giving him strength when the will to live ebbed low. Sometimes they talked together for hours; sometimes the captain would hold his hand while he slept (I remember that once he held it for fourteen hours, afraid that if he withdrew his hand Donald would wake); and at last he had his reward. After a fortnight of hovering on the borderline between life and death, young Ross took a turn for the better. He announced one morning that if we made him a pair of crutches he'd try to walk. He had made the effort. That was all that was needed. From then on though his recovery was painfully slow, he never looked back.

While Ross was nursing his son, Somerville and I set to work on stretcher and sledge. Both proved unexpectedly easy to build: for the whalebone—tough, pliable and light —was about the most suitable material we could have wished for.

Three weeks after Freyja's death, Donald Ross was well enough to be moved; stretcher and sledge were made; and we were ready to go.

I'll never forget the scene as we set out in the pale half-light of the dawn. We hauled the sledge up the cliff to a half-way spur, behind which the bay disappeared from view. Here we paused. And as, for the last time, we looked back into the graveyard of the whales, the sun rose in a blaze of glory over the distant pack ice. Its rays, magnified and refracted like light in a prism, came pouring into the bay in a flood of gold. To start with, the rays didn't reach the foot of the cliffs except in one place, where, by an odd chance of refraction, a single beam slashed swordlike the width of the beach.

And in the path of this single beam was silhouetted a cairn of stones surmounted by a rough whalebone cross; the grave under which we had buried Freyja's locket—her passport to another and I hope a better world. For several seconds the cross blazed out, ashimmer in gold, bright as a flame against a backdrop of velvet. Then the shaft of light moved on, the cross vanished, and we turned our backs on the graveyard and all that was past and headed for home.

18

The Reward

OUR journey back to Winter Harbour was, to put it mildly, difficult and arduous in the extreme. In fact, it would be idle to pretend that it hasn't, in the Arctic, become something of a legend. For we had no fuel for a fire, no gun, no dogs and no tent; in fact, we had nothing except our sledge, our whale-cuts, our sextant and compass and the clothes we stood up in. If it hadn't been for Captain Ross, who was a tower of strength in every emergency, we should never have made it. As it was we headed back in a great curve, giving the north of Prince Patrick Island and the men with yellow hair a wide berth; and after a journey of eight weeks and nearly four hundred miles, we sighted the corrugated roof of the Factor's cabin. No ship after storm ever made a more welcome landfall; and we sighted it in the nick of time—with our stock of food reduced to a half-dozen whale-cuts apiece.

We found, not surprisingly, that the Factor had long ago given us up for lost; that our next-of-kin had been told we were missing, and that our Sea Otter had been sold for scrap. But we didn't care. Just to be back in "civilization" was joy enough; just to have blankets to sleep in, warm water to wash in, hot food to eat, the radio to listen to, and—above all—to have another white man to whom we could recount our strange adventures. All this was not far short of heaven.

We spent three weeks at Winter Harbour, slowly building up our strength. And we needed to; for we found that between the four of us we had lost nearly a dozen stone in weight, and, in addition, both Ross and Somerville were partially snow-blind. Then—on Midsummer Day—we were flown by Piper Cub to Montreal.

And at this point I think I had better bring my story to a close. For the rest is anticlimax, the froth churned up in the wake of our strange adventures: Donald's six weeks in the Mount Royal Hospital (where they broke and re-set his leg); our interviews with the Royal Canadian Mounted Police and the Commissioner for the North West Territories; our negotiations with the whaling company: and finally the parting of the ways—the Rosses going back to England, Somerville returning to McGill University, and I going back to Pangnirtung to my doctor-friend in the Grenfell Mission, in whose house I have spent the last few months writing this account of our adventures.

And, in retrospect, how incredible those adventures seem! Sometimes, as I sit looking out over the peaceful waters of Lancaster Sound, I can hardly believe that everything I have set down really happened. And yet, as I look about me, there is ample proof that it did. My paper-weight is a block of ambergris; my pen is the best that money can buy, and my clothes are tailor-made: for I'm a rich man now. And here, as I write, comes further proof: our Eskimo postman is handing me a letter from England, and I recognize the handwriting. It is Captain Ross's.

His letter speaks for itself, so I quote it in full:

> *"Landfall"*
> *Bridport*
> *Dorset*
> *October 30th, 1959*

My dear Keith,

I promised to let you know as soon as things were all tied-up with Kinross and Jameson. Well, I'm almost afraid to tell you what they say; it seems too good to be true. It appears that the ambergris is the very finest quality (worth a cool £8 an ounce) and for just the lot we brought back they are prepared to offer us £550,000; while for details of the exact location of the graveyard they are prepared to offer us each a further £550,000 or else £100,000 cash down plus a seat on their board (which would, of course, entitle us to a share in the Company's profits once the graveyard is opened up).

Now you must come home, Keith, to see about these things yourself. You have done your day's work, and have money enough now to settle down. There's a place near here for sale which would suit you down to the ground. So do come. If not for good, then at least for a Christmas reunion with Donald and Somerville, both of whom will be here.

And talking of Donald, you wanted to know how he was. Physically he's fine, his leg has mended well, and he's practically lost his limp. But he's still very down in the mouth about Freyja. I don't think he'll ever forget her, and I'll never cease to reproach myself for what happened on Prince Patrick Island. But what's done is done and cannot be undone, and maybe one day he'll find a girl who doesn't mind a ménage à trois with a ghost.

But all this, my old friend, is something I needn't worry you over. I'll save the rest of the news until I see you. And that I hope will be soon.

> *Yours ever,*
>
> *Anthony.*

I've looked up the sailings to Quebec and there's a boat at the end of the month. If I caught that I could be at "Landfall" for Christmas.

I think I'll go. I've had my fill of trapping and whaling and searching for gold, and I'm fairly sick of adventures. I'll buy a cottage that looks out over the Channel, and end my days as every sailor longs to: among friends, watching other people going to sea.

> KEITH ROGERS

Pangnirtung, Baffin Island. July 1959
Bridport, Dorset. February 1960

THE BIG BESTSELLERS
ARE AVON BOOKS!

The Secret Life of Plants			
Peter Tompkins and Christopher Bird	19901	$1.95
The Wildest Heart			
Rosemary Rogers	20529	$1.75
Come Nineveh, Come Tyre			
Allen Drury	19026	$1.75
World Without End, Amen			
Jimmy Breslin	19042	$1.75
The Amazing World of Kreskin			
Kreskin	19034	$1.50
The Oath			
Elie Wiesel	19083	$1.75
A Different Woman			
Jane Howard	19075	$1.95
The Alchemist			
Les Whitten	19919	$1.75
Rule Britannia			
Daphne du Maurier	19547	$1.50
Play of Darkness			
Irving A. Greenfield	19877	$1.50
Facing the Lions			
Tom Wicker	19307	$1.75
High Empire			
Clyde M. Brundy	18994	$1.75
The Wolf and the Dove			
Kathleen E. Woodiwiss	18457	$1.75
Sweet Savage Love			
Rosemary Rogers	17988	$1.75
I'm OK—You're OK			
Thomas A. Harris, M.D.	14662	$1.95
Jonathan Livingston Seagull			
Richard Bach	14316	$1.50

Where better paperbacks are sold, or directly from the publisher. Include 25¢ per copy for mailing; allow three weeks for delivery. Avon Books, Mail Order Dept., 250 West 55th Street, New York, N.Y. 10019

26 WEEKS ON
THE NEW YORK TIMES BESTSELLER LIST

A LITERARY GUILD
FEATURED ALTERNATE

AMERICA'S MOST HONORED WRITER

ThorntonWilder

HIS LATEST,
WONDROUS BESTSELLING NOVEL

Theophilus North

America's celebrated writer explores, through Theophilus
North, the lives of the saints and the sinners, the rich and
the servants, in the Newport, Rhode Island of the '20s.

"EXTRAORDINARILY ENTERTAINING."
The New York Times

19059/$1.75